THE WORLD FAMOUS
·HOTEL ROYALE·

SECRETS
OF A TEENAGE
HEIRESS

Have you read the *It Girl* series,
also by Katy Birchall?

Superstar Geek
Team Awkward
Don't Tell the Bridesmaid

THE WORLD FAMOUS
HOTEL ROYALE

↰ A.K.A my house

SECRETS

OF A TEENAGE

HEIRESS

KATY BIRCHALL

EGMONT

EGMONT

We bring stories to life

First published in paperback in Great Britain 2018
by Egmont UK Limited
The Yellow Building, 1 Nicholas Road, London W11 4AN

Text copyright © 2018 Katy Birchall

The moral rights of the author have been asserted

ISBN 978 1 4052 8650 3

www.egmont.co.uk

67130/1

A CIP catalogue record for this title is available from the British
Library

Typeset by Avon DataSet Ltd, Bidford on Avon, Warwickshire
Printed and bound in Great Britain by the CPI Group

For Sam, Luke and Lily

ONE

Prince Gustav stole my selfie stick.

And now I was stuck hiding in his wardrobe, while his PA attempted to teach him how to strike the perfect pose.

'Instagram is all about confidence,' the PA explained, as Prince Gustav nervously checked his teeth in the nearest mirror. 'Loosen your shoulders and show them some attitude. They want to see the real you.'

I peered through the wardrobe keyhole out into the suite as the PA adjusted MY selfie stick and waited patiently for Prince Gustav to finish rolling his shoulders back and forth.

'Are you ready?'

'I don't know, Freddie.' Prince Gustav sighed dramatically. 'I was sure I wanted an Instagram account but now I feel very stressed about the whole idea.'

'I understand,' Freddie agreed, 'but that's why I'm here to talk you through it. And it's really about time that we had one up and running. Soon you'll be taking selfies wherever you go without any assistance.'

'What do I do with my head?'

'It's all very simple. I've done plenty of research and downloaded all the best apps so we can get the filter just right.' Freddie ushered Prince Gustav nearer to the window. 'First, we need the perfect lighting. There you go, that's great. Now, tilt your head.'

'I feel like a Labrador.'

'It's a great angle,' Freddie insisted and all the security men and women in the room nodded in agreement. 'Perfect! Now, take the selfie stick and when you feel ready, just click that button at the bottom.'

Prince Gustav warily took the end of the pink and silver bejewelled selfie stick and attempted to position it correctly, almost knocking Freddie out as he swung it through the air.

How could he not know how to use a selfie stick? He wasn't even old! Do castles not get Wi-Fi or something?

Ducking swiftly out of the way, Freddie gave the prince an enthusiastic thumbs up. Silence descended upon the room as everyone waited in anticipation. Keeping his head in position, Prince Gustav tweaked his shirt collar with his free hand before clearing his throat and forming his lips into a mild pout. After a few seconds, there was a small click.

'Did it work?' Prince Gustav asked, swinging the stick clumsily back towards Freddie.

Freddie unclipped the phone and everyone held their breath as he inspected the photo.

'Well,' he said, breaking into a wide grin and holding out the screen so Prince Gustav could see. 'I'd call that a royal whopper!'

'Not bad for my first selfie!' Prince Gustav exclaimed. 'Let's do another!'

Oh. My. God. This literally could not get worse.

I guess this whole tragic scenario made me look bad because *technically* I had broken into the hotel suite of Prince Gustav, but he started it – he 'borrowed' my selfie stick without permission, which, if we're going to get technical, was actually Mum's fault because she took it upon herself to lend it to him without saying a word to me. And it is MY selfie stick, not hers to just give away to whomever she likes, so that counts as THEFT.

'Matthew!' I had shouted earlier, slightly out of breath from running full pelt across the lobby. I almost dropped Fritz, my dachshund, as I slid across the marble floor, stabilising myself on the reception desk.

I rang the gold bell vigorously. 'Matthew!'

'What's wrong with *you*?'

Urgh. Cal Weston, Matthew's annoying son was sitting on top of the far end of the desk, watching me curiously. He was in the year above me at school, not that we ever spoke there. I couldn't seem to avoid him in the hotel, though, he was always lurking around like some kind of weirdo. What kind of loser spends their free time at the place where their parent works?

OK, so technically I do, but I *live* here so it's different.

'None of your business,' I said, ringing the bell again. 'Matthew!'

I caught Cal rolling his eyes.

'You know,' I said, glaring, 'you're not meant to be sitting up there. Guests are arriving all the time and you shouldn't be the first thing they see.'

'But you screeching like that is the first thing they should hear?'

I scowled.

'If I stay sitting up here, are you going to snitch on me?' He sighed, looking back to his laptop screen. 'Like you did last time.'

'I did not snitch!' I protested. 'That was your fault! That peacock was COMPLETELY out of control and . . . oh, never mind. MATTHEW!'

'Can I hold Fritz?'

'No,' I snapped. 'He only likes nice people. MATTHEEEEEEW!'

'Yes?' a calm voice answered behind me, making me jump out of my skin.

'There you are! I've been ringing the bell for a billion years.'

Cal snorted. 'You've been here two minutes.'

I ignored him. 'Matthew, I need to report a crime.'

Matthew raised his eyebrows. 'Oh?' He moved behind the reception desk, straightening his dark green, gold-buttoned uniform. 'Here at Hotel Royale?'

'Yes, here at Hotel Royale,' I said, tapping my nails impatiently on the desk. 'That's why I'm telling you and not the police. Someone's been into my room and stolen my selfie stick. The one Vivienne Westwood designed for me especially.'

I ignored Cal's snigger.

'What is all this racket?' Audrey, the general manager, came clacking across the reception hall in her polished stilettos. 'Flick, I thought you were meant to be doing your homework upstairs.'

I rolled my eyes. Even though she's not my mum, Audrey sure acts like it. She is so good at bossing everyone about in the hotel that the queen once tried to hire her to boss everyone about at Buckingham Palace instead, but she turned down the job to stay here. Which I guess was good for my mum and everything, because she didn't lose her manager, but it also meant that I'm stuck with Audrey watching me like a hawk.

'I was just telling Matthew that I have been the victim of a heinous crime.'

Cal let out a loud 'HA!' and shook his head.

I narrowed my eyes at him. 'Don't you have anywhere better to be?'

'And miss this entertainment? Are you kidding? I've got a front-row seat here.'

Fritz began to scrabble about impatiently in my arms, so I plonked him on top of the reception desk. It was so polished that when he tried to walk along it, his legs kept slipping and sliding, like Bambi on ice. If I hadn't been so distressed about my selfie stick, it would have been hilarious.

'No, Flick!' Audrey scolded, snatching Fritz and holding him at arm's length, so his back legs were just flailing about in the air. Audrey has never really had a way with dogs. 'What have I told you about putting Fritz on the reception desk? Take him off.'

'I'll take him!' Cal offered. She handed him over quickly and promptly checked her suit thoroughly for dog hairs even though he hadn't even touched her.

Technically, pets weren't allowed at the Royale but two years ago, after months of my dedicated pestering, Mum had caved. Now Fritz comes with me everywhere, except to school, and even Audrey has admitted that he is particularly handsome 'for a dog'. His social media profile is really growing and the guests love him too. One guest, Mr Dancy, stays at Hotel Royale three or four times a year and he always brings Fritz a new jumper to keep him cosy during the winter months. Today, Fritz was wearing a blue one with 'HOT DOG' printed on the back. He has an extensive collection of knitwear these days.

'Why were you causing a fuss?' Audrey asked, leading me away from some guests who were swanning in through the revolving doors laden with designer shopping bags. Matthew, as head concierge, went over to greet them and ask about their day. Delighted to see him, they immediately launched into a full description of all the sightseeing they'd done and a dull story about one of them getting stuck in a telephone box. Poor Matthew always has to pretend to enjoy these boring, repetitive conversations and he's been working here FOREVER, like, fifteen years. He laughed and gasped in all the right places. He was very convincing. Mum should really give him a raise for this daily torture.

'Flick?' Audrey prompted, as I watched him distractedly. 'What's going on?'

'Oh yeah, right. So, my selfie stick has been stolen. It's very important. Fritz always uploads a new photo to his Instagram account at 5.30 p.m. on the dot and the selfie stick is key to the whole operation.'

'Fritz uses the selfie stick?' Audrey looked confused.

'Of course not! It's for the angles, it's to do with the allegory.' I sighed. 'You wouldn't understand. The important thing is to find it before 5.30 so I can post his next picture, otherwise we'll be letting down *thousands* of people. Forty-five thousand, to be exact.'

'I see.' Audrey smiled. 'I think I know what's happened here. You need to speak to your mother.' She checked her watch. 'She will have just finished a meeting and has five minutes until the next one. Let me give her a call, wait here.'

She marched back to the reception desk and into the office behind it. A few moments later, she reappeared. 'She'll be with you in a moment. Why don't you take a seat?'

She gestured to the purple velvet armchairs in the corners of the reception hall. I gladly took Fritz back from the evil clutches of Cal, and sat him on one of the armchairs while I nestled into the other one. As we waited, Fritz sat up regally on the plush velvet, enjoying the adoring waves he received from guests coming into the hotel.

When we were little, Cal and I used to sit in these armchairs for ages, spying on all the guests, whispering made-up stories about who each person was and what they did, and then laughing our heads off, until Audrey would come along and shoo us away. That was obviously a *long* time ago, when Cal wasn't such a weirdo and we were friends.

FINALLY Mum came down the grand staircase, already looking impatient. She always looks impatient when it comes to me, even though I'm her only child and therefore should be the sole reason for her being.

I reminded her of that the other day, when she was annoyed with me for setting off all the smoke alarms in the hotel because I'd put a pizza in the oven but got distracted by YouTube videos of dogs eating peanut butter and forgot about it. Firstly, it was her fault for NEVER letting me order room service even though we live in a hotel with a Michelin-star chef, and secondly, most parents would have been thrilled that their beloved child was showing an interest in cooking at the delicate age of fourteen. But *noooooo*, I got in big trouble just because all the guests and staff had to be evacuated and it made the news headlines because everyone thought there had been this big fire in the grandest hotel in London. The PR team had to work through the night persuading guests and members of the press that everything was fine and it was in fact all down to a pizza, which now resembled a lump of coal, on the fifteenth floor.

As Mum walked towards me, I could kind of see what people mean when they say that she has this authoritative aura about her. Just the way she walks in and sits down seems to command the attention of a room. I don't think I've ever seen her slump or look scruffy. Even at weekends, she dresses as though she might be going to a meeting at any minute. I also think a lot of her power comes from the fact that she never raises her voice. Ever. Even that time when Cal and I let that goat loose in the ballroom, or last week with the pizza thing. When she's disappointed or angry, she just gives you this look and it makes your insides go icy cold.

Believe me, I've been on the receiving end of that look WAY too many times.

'Would it be possible to remove Fritz so that I might sit down? Perhaps he could sit on your lap,' she suggested, sharing a knowing look with Audrey who was watching us, bemused, from behind the reception desk.

'He likes having the chair to himself.'

'Flick,' Mum said in a warning tone.

'Fine.' I sighed. 'But if he gets angry, I'm blaming you.'

'I am happy to take full responsibility.'

I got up and slid my hands under Fritz's belly to lift him from the chair. He growled immediately. 'I tried telling her,' I said to him under my breath.

'I hear you've been asking about your selfie stick?' Mum said calmly, sitting down in the armchair as Fritz settled on my lap.

'Yes, it has been stolen. Potentially by an overzealous fan of Fritz's. I suggest we close down the hotel and search all the rooms. We should start with the opera singer on the third floor. I don't trust anyone who wears a wig that big.'

'That won't be necessary, Flick,' Mum said, before standing up again to greet a waiter passing by, on his way to the kitchen.

'Good afternoon, Ms Royale and Miss Royale. And . . . uh . . . Mr Fritz.'

'Good afternoon, Timothy.' Mum smiled warmly. 'How is that Italian coming along?'

'You remembered! It's going very well, thank you.'

'Wonderful. I always wanted to learn Italian but never quite mastered it,' Mum confessed. 'The furthest I really got was . . . wait for it . . . *spaghetti Bolognese*!'

They both burst into laughter as though Mum had said something genuinely funny.

I really hope Mum hasn't passed her humour gene down to me. It's very niche.

I coughed impatiently.

'Well, I'll leave you to it,' the waiter said, getting the hint, before he scurried off towards the staff lift that went down to the kitchens.

'Amazing, isn't it?' Mum sat back down again. 'A full-time job and he finds time to study because his fiancé is Italian and he wants to learn it by the time of the wedding. Very impressive.'

I rolled my eyes. 'OK, Mum, that's very nice and everything, but can we please focus on something actually important? This is serious! Someone's broken into our flat. Potentially a selfie-obsessed opera singer!' I leaned in towards her. 'Now, I'm happy to tell you that I will keep the police out of this and not press charges if the selfie stick is returned safely to me.'

The corner of Mum's mouth twitched. 'How grown up of you, but there's no mystery here and certainly no thief. I lent your selfie stick to a guest. Prince Gustav Xavier III, in fact.'

I blinked at her. 'What?'

'I lent your selfie stick to Prince Gustav. You know he's staying here, don't you? In the Sapphire Suite.'

'You lent my selfie stick to some prince? Why would you do that?'

'Matthew overheard him talking to his PA in the lobby.

Apparently he bought one in Duty Free but misplaced it. He seemed distressed so Matthew informed me of the situation and I offered him yours so they wouldn't have to go to the trouble of purchasing another. Plus,' she added, winking at Audrey, 'Prince Gustav is rather handsome.'

'Mum! Gross! And that selfie stick is mine and Fritz's!'

'The prince only needs it for today. His PA promised they would return it tomorrow. I had one of the staff leave it in his room about an hour ago, ready for his return from afternoon tea with his aunt.'

'But what about me?'

'What about you?'

'I need it!'

'I'm sure you can cope without it for one evening.'

'No way! Not only does Fritz have to prep for his Instagram post, but I was planning on doing a practice run of a vlog today and I need the selfie stick to test all the angles.'

'Vlog?' Mum raised her eyebrows.

Here we go.

'I thought we discussed this, Flick,' Mum said sternly. 'I was very clear about my opinion.'

'Yes, you were. And I've taken your thoughts into consideration.'

The corner of Mum's mouth twitched again. 'And?'

'And I've decided they're void.'

'Flick,' Mum began in her best warning tone.

'Mum, look, all my friends agree that I would gain millions of followers like *that* –' I clicked my fingers for effect – 'if I started vlogging. All the other heiresses are doing it. At my age most of them have handbag and perfume ranges, thanks to their online profiles. I'm fourteen years old now; you have to let me do my own thing. You know, like in *The Little Mermaid*.'

'The Disney film?' Mum looked baffled. 'What's that got to do with vlogging?'

'Duh. Her dad is all clingy and so she leaves him to go and live with the hot prince. You know, Mum, you could learn a lot from King Triton's mistakes.'

'Hi, Christine.'

I sighed dramatically as Cal came over, his laptop nestled under his arm. Why was he always butting in?

'Hello, Callum,' Mum said brightly. 'How are you?'

'Good, I was just on my way to see Chef. I hear he's got a new strawberry mousse on the menu.'

'He does, it's outstanding.' Mum turned to me. 'Have you tried the new mousse?'

'I don't care about mousse!' I cried. 'What about my selfie stick?'

'Trust me, this mousse is to die for.' Mum turned back

to Cal, completely ignoring my distress. 'I hear you came top of the class again in your English paper?'

Cal blushed. 'Dad told you, huh? It was only one essay, it's not a big deal.'

'He's very proud of you, and so he should be. You always were very hard-working.'

I couldn't help but notice Mum direct a wistful glance towards me as she said that.

Which was very unfair considering I would be just as hard-working if SOMEONE didn't go around lending random princes my selfie stick and thus keeping me from uploading said hard work.

'Still hoping to be a journalist some day?'

'That's the big plan.'

'I can introduce you to Nicholas Huntley, if you'd like,' Mum continued. Cal's eyes widened.

'Why would you want to meet *him*?' I crossed my arms, annoyed that the conversation was moving away from the problem in hand. 'Isn't he just the guy who married that actress, Helena Montaine?'

Hotel Royale was one of Helena Montaine's favourite places to dine, so she was often here for big meetings with famous directors or with her new husband, Nicholas Huntley, and her daughter and step-daughter, the It Girls Marianne Montaine and Anna Huntley. It was always a big deal when they were in the building, as there would be hordes of paparazzi outside waiting to get a photo. Famous people stay at the hotel all the time, but Mum was particularly friendly with Helena and her husband. I often saw her enjoying a drink with them in the cocktail bar, talking about really boring topics that no one cares about, like the news and stuff.

'Nicholas Huntley happens to be the greatest journalist of all time,' Cal said pompously. 'And he's written some of the most important books about war weaponry there have ever been. His book on tanks won the Baillie Gifford Prize.'

I yawned as he finished his sentence. There is seriously no one in the world as boring as Cal Weston. Except maybe this Nicholas Huntley person and his tank books.

'Tell me, Callum,' Mum said, abruptly standing up and straightening her white tailored jacket. 'Do you spend your evenings vlogging?'

'Uh.' Cal looked confused. 'No. It's not really my thing.'

'You see, Flick?' Mum looked back down at me. 'Cal doesn't vlog.'

'That's because he has nothing interesting to say,' I protested, as Cal rolled his eyes. 'It's me the people want to know about.'

'We'll talk about this later. You'll have to do without

the selfie stick for one night. And so will Fritz.'

'But Mu–'

'End of discussion, Flick,' Mum said firmly. 'Now, I've got another meeting to get to. Good to see you, Callum. Keep up the hard work.'

She patted Cal on the shoulder and walked back across the reception hall and through the revolving doors to her car waiting outside.

'You're starting a vlog?' Cal sniggered. 'About what?'

'About my life,' I huffed. 'Not that it's any of your business.'

'Why would anyone want to know about your life?'

'Excuse me, I featured on the *Daily Post*'s "50 Heirs to Watch" list. So there.'

'Yeah, you came in at number forty-nine,' he said as he walked away. 'Real impressive.'

I glared at his back, then stomped loudly towards the lift with Fritz, ignoring the raised eyebrows of Audrey and Matthew, and prodded the button for Floor 15. Leaning against the back mirror of the lift, I cuddled Fritz as the blinking light passed the other floor numbers.

The whole thing was completely ridiculous and totally unfair. Just because Prince Gustav Xavier III is a prince, it doesn't mean he can go around stealing stuff. And, what's more, HE'S NOT EVEN A REAL PRINCE! The monarchy in his country hasn't properly existed since FOREVER, but he still swans about the place using the 'prince' title, going to the best parties and stealing other people's selfie sticks.

That was when the idea hit me. He wasn't actually using the selfie stick right now because he was at afternoon tea with his aunt! Mum had said it had been left out for him for when he got back. So I could sneak into his suite, grab the selfie stick, take it back to my room for Fritz's photo shoot and then if Prince Gustav needed it later, he could come and ask and I might be inclined to lend it to him. I congratulated myself out loud to Fritz on such an excellent plan. He barked in agreement.

All I had to do was break into Mum's office in the flat and get hold of her master key, which opens every room in the hotel. And that was a doddle. I'd had a key cut for her office without her knowing when I was nine. I would be in and out of Prince Gustav's room in a matter of seconds without anyone noticing. Easy.

Obviously now that I was hiding inside Prince Gustav's wardrobe while he pouted in what he referred to as a 'mysterious yet alluring way', I regretted that decision.

I had been so close to victory. I'd had the selfie stick in my hands when I heard a booming voice echoing down the corridor. I had run to the door to check through the peephole and, sure enough, there was Prince Gustav, striding towards me, arguing with one of his many security guards about the pros and cons of social media.

I quickly threw the selfie stick back down and, after running about the room in a panic, I clambered into the wardrobe and crouched back as far as possible.

Attempting to get comfortable without making any noise, I realised that the chances of my mum finding out about this were really quite high. If Prince Gustav decided to don different outfits for his new Instagram account, which, judging by his levels of enthusiasm, was highly likely, I was busted.

My only hope was that Prince Gustav might have to rush off to a party or something, leaving the coast clear.

'Keep this up, Your Royal Highness, and you'll have more Instagram followers by the end of the day than all the Kardashians put together!'

I sighed as Prince Gustav pulled the bouquet of flowers out of the vase on the dressing table and struck a rose-sniffing pose.

'Very creative, Your Highness!' Freddie cheered. 'Something for the ladies!'

That was when disaster struck.

The dulcet tones of Fritz's high-pitched bark went off in my pocket: my text alert. I had forgotten to put my phone on silent and I was suddenly getting a flurry of messages. Who was texting me this much? I reached for my phone but it was too late.

I heard quick footsteps and someone yell, 'GET BACK, YOUR HIGHNESS,' before the wardrobe doors were dramatically swung open and I found myself squinting up at the prince's burly security men.

'Hi,' I squeaked, ducking my head to look through their legs at Prince Gustav, who was standing against the back wall with a security guard shielding him, the selfie stick still swinging from his hand and the flowers scattered all over the floor. 'Welcome to Hotel Royale, Prince Gustav. I'm Flick.'

He blinked back at me in shocked silence.

'Great pictures, by the way. Instagram won't know what's hit it.'

Yep. Mum was definitely going to kill me.

TWO

Flick! OMG I had to text you straight away. You'll never believe what just happened to me! Are you there?

Flick? Are you there? Helloooooo!

OK, I'll just tell you anyway. I was just in the garden talking to Mum and A BIRD LANDED ON MY HEAD

Seriously, it just landed right on there!!! I didn't even have any food on my head or anything, it just perched there! According to Dad it was a sparrow. I'll send you all the pics now! Mum took a hundred of them! Enjoy!

Hey Grace, sorry for the late reply.

> Got myself in a bit of an awkward
> situation here involving a prince.
> Talk later

> OMG your life is so cool compared to mine.
> You're hanging out with royalty and I've spent
> the evening with a bird on my head!! Oh well.
> At least it didn't poop in my hair! See you at school!

'Fan. Demand?'

That's how my mum spoke those words, as though there was a full stop between them. She always speaks like that when she's really angry – no long sentences but every word coming out of her mouth is said veeeeery slooooooowly to make sure her victim feels as nervous as possible. Luckily, I'm pretty immune to that tone these days.

'Yes.' I nodded, folding my arms and wondering how long this was going to take. This whole selfie-stick debacle had taken up most of my evening already.

Mum looked at Audrey and Matthew – both of whom were standing a few metres away watching the proceedings – supposedly to see if either of them had any comments at this stage. Neither of them said anything, so she turned back to face me.

Fritz was there too, lying across my feet, which is this weird thing he does. I don't mind it because if I'm not wearing shoes it keeps my feet warm, which is handy, but sometimes I forget he's there and get up to do something and he suddenly tips off and goes rolling across the floor. I would find those occasions funny if he didn't get in such a strop with me afterwards.

'Just so I'm clear,' Mum began, leaning back on her desk, '"fan demand" is . . . your explanation?'

'Yeah.' I shrugged. 'Otherwise none of this would have happened.'

'What. Do. You. Mean?'

'I tried explaining this to you earlier but you refused to listen.' I sighed. 'I had to upload a new post on to Fritz's Instagram feed at 5.30 p.m. That's when I had promised his legion of fans that the next photo would be up. I didn't want to let them down! It would be like that time Matthew promised he'd get me front-row tickets for Cirque du Soleil at the last minute but it wasn't his *priority* and I ended up in Row F behind some stupid lady with a topknot.'

Matthew gave a small cough. I smiled graciously at him.

'Don't worry, Matthew, you forgive and forget.'

'Go. On. With. The. Story,' Mum growled. Seriously, someone get the lady a Strepsil.

'Well, I couldn't upload the photo without the selfie stick. It just wouldn't have worked with the rest of the vibe of Fritz's feed. It's very specific and artistic. And I didn't have any appropriate stock photos I could use instead. So I was just going to pop in to see Prince Gustav, ask for the selfie stick for five minutes and that would be that! But he wasn't there.'

'So you just . . . decided to break in and steal it?' Mum asked slowly.

'You know, when you say it like that, it really sounds a lot worse than it was. I mean, *technically* Prince Gustav stole the stick from me.'

Mum closed her eyes for a moment and let out a long, deep sigh.

Seizing the opportunity, I pulled out my phone, checking for messages. Thankfully there were no more photos of Grace with a bird on her head. There was just one from Ella reminding me that I'd borrowed her mascara at school yesterday and could she have it back. Ella can be so whiny when she wants to be. Which is a LOT of the time.

'I guess we're done here,' I said, preparing to stand up.

'Not. Quite.'

I slumped back into the seat. Mum walked slowly around the desk to sit down in the large leather chair behind it. She put her head back and looked up at the ceiling before ever so slowly lowering her eyes back down to meet mine. Talk about dramatic.

'Mum, I really have to get back to my friend. It's important.' I waved my phone about.

'I'm sure the important business of a fourteen-year-old can wait while we try to get to the bottom of why you took it upon yourself to break into Prince Gustav's hotel room.'

'I told you, to get my selfie stick. Mum, were you even listening? I just explained the whole thing.'

'Did I or did I not ask you to do without it. For. One. Night?'

'I was going to put it back,' I pointed out. 'Mum, no offence, but you're kind of overreacting.'

Mum pinched the top of her nose, which is a signal that she is concentrating. Hard.

It is highly dangerous to interrupt her when she is pinching the top of her nose. I know this because I once interrupted her pinching the top of her nose at a cashpoint. She'd had a mind blank about her PIN and all I did was point out that she was being really embarrassing standing in the street, pinching the top of her nose.

According to her, she had been *this close* to remembering her pin but my 'loud' interruption had disturbed her and so her card got swallowed. She spent the next few days droning on and on about how frustrating it was to be waiting for a new debit card and then giving me pointed looks. The word 'scapegoat' comes to mind.

Whatever, I selflessly let that one go. But I know now never to interrupt the weird, nose-pinching thing.

I began texting Ella back while I waited for Mum to conclude her nose-pinching, but stopped when Audrey gave a not-so-subtle 'ahem', and waggled her eyebrows at me. I put my phone back in my pocket.

'I want you to listen to me very carefully, Felicity,' Mum began, lowering her hand and opening her eyes. 'You are going to go and see Prince Gustav – NOT when you decide, Audrey will book an appointment with him – and you will be on time for the appointment and you will apologise profusely for your behaviour and assure him that nothing like this will *ever* happen again. Is that clear?'

'Crystal. Audrey, let me know a time that suits. Can I go now?'

'I'm. Not. Finished.' Mum clasped her hands together, resting them on the desk. 'You will be grounded for two weeks.'

'WHAT?' I sat upright, disturbing Fritz who snarled

loudly. 'You can't do that! It's Ella's party next week!'

'I can do that, and you're lucky it's only two weeks and not longer. In addition, you will help around the hotel in whatever way Audrey and Matthew see fit. If you're going to be stuck here every evening, you might as well make yourself useful.'

'Are you serious?' I looked at her in disbelief. 'Like . . . *chores*?'

Audrey stifled a laugh. Traitor.

'Yes, chores. I suggest you begin by helping the catering team in the kitchen. I'm sure they have some dishes that need washing. You can start right now.'

'Well, what am I supposed to tell Ella?' I huffed. 'She was counting on me going to her party.'

'You can tell her that your mother is punishing you because you broke into the room of Prince Gustav Xavier III and you're lucky he's not pressing charges.' She stood up and gestured towards the door, indicating the end of the conversation. 'I'm sure Ella will be able to handle your absence from her party with grace and understanding.'

I snorted.

Clearly, Mum had never met Ella before. Last time she invited me to one of her 'exclusive' sleepovers, I couldn't go because my aunt was over from New York. I've never been invited to one again.

'What about Fritz?' I argued, after the party plea didn't work.

'What *about* Fritz?'

'I need to walk him and stuff.'

'You can fit that in around your chores. Or you can ask Jamie if he will kindly take him on an extra-long walk during the day.'

Jamie was one of the sommeliers and also Fritz's daytime walker. He was mad about dogs and offered to walk Fritz when Mum had just bought him and was working out what to do with him while I was at school. Apparently, Jamie likes to discuss the new wines he introduces to the menu with Fritz on his daily walks to the park – it helps him remember all the details about the vintages and vineyards.

'Audrey,' Mum continued, 'if you could accompany Flick down to the kitchens and explain the situation to Chef, I would be very grateful. I have to make an appearance at an event in the ballroom. And if someone could pick her up from the kitchen and escort her back to our flat in an hour, I would also appreciate it.'

'I am not a child,' I hissed, sweeping Fritz up from the floor into my arms, and stomping to the door.

Mum raised her eyebrows. 'You could have fooled me.'

THREE

Audrey waited for me to drop Fritz back off at the flat and then walked me down to the kitchen. Chef was running around trying to prepare everything for dinner and, after a brief word with Audrey, he welcomed me to his team and pointed at the pile of dirty pots stacked next to a large sink in the far corner.

'You'll be out of everyone's way there.' He smiled, with a wink at Audrey.

I shot them both a dirty look before Chef gave me the thumbs up and sped off to season a sauce. Audrey put her hand on my shoulder.

'It's not that bad,' she said soothingly. 'I'll be back for you in an hour. Try to stay out of trouble until then.'

I shook her hand off and stropped over to the sink, eyeing up the repulsive neon orange washing-up gloves. I held one of them up for inspection.

'Ew.' I sniffed and looked around. A young chef was rushing past holding a ladle. 'Excuse me!' She came to a screeching halt.

'Yes?'

'Are these the only gloves you have?'

'Sorry?'

'For the washing-up,' I explained impatiently. 'Don't you have any other types? Any other colours?'

'No, those are the ones we all use.'

'Fine.' I slapped the gloves down on the side. 'I just won't use them.'

'Uh.' She looked about, unsure. 'We . . . we have to use them. It's health and safety.'

'They're disgusting. I'm not using them.'

'Put those on, please, Flick, no argument! You don't want me to report bad behaviour to the boss, do you?' Chef appeared out of nowhere. 'Ah, there you are, Sasha. I've been waiting on that ladle. Come along, we mustn't disturb Flick. She has a big job with those pots.'

Sasha shot me a sympathetic look before she scurried after him holding up the ladle dutifully. I should have known Chef Kian would find this all one big joke; he always liked a good laugh at my expense. I carefully slid on the orange gloves and, letting out a long drawn-out sigh, I leaned forwards to work out how to turn on the large rinsing tap.

'Well, well, well, look who it is.'

I reluctantly turned to face Cal Weston, who was

grinning gleefully at me, a spoon in one hand and a bowl of strawberry mousse in the other.

'It's been a while since you graced the kitchens with your presence.'

'Stalking is a crime, you know,' I said angrily, reaching for the washing-up liquid. 'It's sad that you just follow me around.'

'I was here first. If anyone's following anyone, it's you following me.'

'Why are you even down here? Don't you ever go home?'

'The kitchen is the best place to be. It's the land of free food.' He took a large mouthful of mousse. 'We used to hang out here all the time before you got too good for it.'

'I did not get too good for it, I just got a life.' I began to scrub the biggest pot in the pile. 'Unlike some people I know.'

'Ouch! You are such a hothead.'

'I am NOT a hothead,' I seethed. Cal always teased me about being a hot-tempered redhead, even though I continually corrected him that my hair wasn't red, it was auburn. And at least my hair looked like it had been brushed once in a while, unlike the bird's nest he was sporting on top of his head.

'I heard on the grapevine that you have an appointment with Prince Gustav,' he commented.

I scrubbed harder at the stubborn grease around the side of the pot. 'That's right. He's trying to suck up to me so he can get an invite to the Christmas Ball.'

'Oh, the Christmas Ball. Nothing to do with you having to apologise about hiding in his wardrobe then?'

I ignored him and concentrated on my impossible task. The washing-up was going to take me all night at this rate.

'I need a favour.'

I laughed, not bothering to look up. 'Are you serious?'

'Yes.'

The sincerity of Cal's voice took me by surprise. I turned to look at him and saw he was watching me carefully, an earnest expression on his face. I put down the pot, turned off the tap and folded my arms, pretending not to care that the washing-up liquid mixed with water and grease was now dripping from the gloves down my clothes.

'What favour?'

'It's for a competition I'm entering.' He put down the bowl and got out his phone, showing me the website page for Young Journalist of the Year. 'I need to write a feature that will stand out. The winners are announced just before Christmas.'

'So? What's that got to do with me?'

'An interview with Prince Gustav would *definitely* stand out. Maybe you could mention it to him when you go for this meeting,' he said hopefully.

I burst out laughing and swivelled back to the sink, turning on the tap and picking up the pot again.

'What's so funny?' he asked, shoving his phone into his pocket.

'Well, for one thing, you're a teenager, so the chances of Prince Gustav giving you an exclusive interview are slim. And for another thing, you've spent the whole day – no, wait, the last few years – being rude to me, so I'm not going to risk looking like an idiot in front of him for you.'

'I think you managed to look like an idiot in front of him all by yourself today,' he snapped.

'I know, why don't you write a feature about hanging out at a hotel for no reason, getting in everyone's way and annoying everyone in sight?'

He didn't say anything as I reached for more washing-up liquid, squirting as much as possible across the pot until the sink was full of bubbles.

'Forget I said anything,' he said quietly, picking up his bowl and turning away.

'Cal, wait.'

He stopped.

'Don't say anything at school about me washing-up,

OK?' I shook some bubbles off the gloves. 'It's not exactly a great look.'

He glared down at the floor and shook his head before walking off. I had no idea if that meant he'd tell people or not, but I wasn't that worried. Even if he did it's not like anyone would listen.

My arm got tired from all the scrubbing so I turned off the water and pulled off the gloves. I wiped my brow and looked down at my handiwork. Somehow I had managed to splash water everywhere and I hadn't even finished one pot. How does anyone have the time for this sort of thing?

I looked at my phone in case I had any messages: none. I put it down on the side and looked around to find something else to distract me. I spotted a door a few metres from where I was and remembered that it used to be some sort of pantry. Chef would always find me sitting in there in my pyjamas, stuffing myself with chocolate. I smiled as I remembered how I used to try to pretend I'd accidentally locked myself in there, but the chocolate all over my hands would give me away. Chef found it hilarious and would slip me a cookie before sending me back upstairs to bed.

I checked that no one was looking in my direction – they were all busy running around, paying no attention to me. I crept over to the door and pulled it open. Just as I remembered, it was lined with shelves bursting with baking supplies, and at the back there was a massive chocolate cake. Moving forwards to inspect the cake properly, the door, which had been propped open with the back of my foot, shut behind me. I tried the light switch but the bulb must have been broken. I went to push open the door again but it wouldn't budge.

Oh no.

I threw all my weight against the door but it was firmly shut. I cursed myself for leaving my phone on the side; I could have really used the torch.

'Hello? Chef?' I called out, pressed against the door.

No one came.

Feeling my way to the back of the pantry, I sat down and waited. I put my head in my hands. This was a disaster. Chef would tell Mum and who knows what sort of job she might give me next? Spider catcher? Shower cleaner? Listen to Matthew talk about the room booking system? I shuddered and hoped that that Sasha person might come this way again looking for another ladle, realise that I was gone and put two and two together. She seemed nice. A problem-solver.

After a few minutes of nothing happening, the thought crossed my mind that I might actually die in this pantry.

How depressing.

In order for that not to happen any time soon I would need sustenance and I could smell the chocolate cake on the shelf, right next to my head. I carefully felt for the silver tray that it was sitting on and pulled it out to place it gently on the floor. There was no doubt that this cake was for some kind of occasion or event – Chef wouldn't just be keeping a cake in here for no reason. I would have to make sure I didn't spoil it. I remembered that when I'd seen it from the door, there had been some kind of message on the top layer, spelled out in small white chocolate buttons. With my eyes adjusting to the dark, I could make out the white buttons scattered across the top. I began to pick a few off, careful not to take too many, confident that Chef wouldn't notice a few less chocolate buttons. They were delicious.

Suddenly the door swung open and light poured into the room. 'And in here, Boss, is the polo team cake itself!'

I heard gasps and then my mum's voice broke the silence. 'Flick?'

'I don't believe it,' said Chef, aghast. 'Some things never change.'

I blinked up at them. 'Finally! I was running out of oxygen.'

I scrambled to my feet.

'Someone needs to fix that light,' I instructed. 'And

what is the point of having ugly washing-up gloves for health and safety, if you have dodgy doors that lock people in pantries?'

'You just turn the handle,' Chef explained, looking confused.

I glanced down at the door handle. I could have sworn it hadn't been there before. But then I didn't remember searching the door, just pushing against it. Whoops. Oh well, I'd better run with it.

'It's broken,' I insisted. 'Anyway, I'll get back to my washing-up now. I was really getting into it.'

I darted past Mum to the sink and began to battle with the washing-up gloves again. After a few moments, I heard footsteps behind me.

'Flick, would you mind turning round for a moment, please?'

I grimaced at Mum's stern tone and slowly swivelled to face her.

The cake had been placed on top of the work surface and Mum was standing on one side of it with her arms crossed and Chef was standing on the other with his hands on his hips, a team of young chefs gathering behind him.

'Hey, everyone.' I waved my glove slightly over-enthusiastically, spraying Chef with water. 'Oops, sorry.'

I laughed. Chef did not laugh back. He wiped his face with the back of his sleeve.

'What's up?' I asked innocently.

'Well, you see, Chef and his pastry team have been toiling long and hard to create this splendid cake for Great Britain's polo team. They have an important tournament coming up and they're holding a party for it this evening here at the Royale, in the ballroom.'

'Cool.' I nodded. 'Good luck to them.'

'Interesting choice of words,' Mum said calmly. 'Chef, would you be so kind as to inform my daughter what the top of the cake said after you painstakingly arranged mini chocolate buttons to spell it out in an intricate calligraphy style?'

'"Good Luck, Polo Team",' Chef grumbled.

'Thank you, Chef. Flick, did you, by any chance, help yourself to some of the chocolate buttons when you were stuck in the pantry for all of five minutes?'

'I may have had a few,' I admitted. 'I didn't know how long I was going to be in there! I thought I might starve!'

Sasha let out a giggle and I smiled at her gratefully. Anything to lighten the atmosphere. She stopped quickly though after a sharp look from Chef.

Mum continued. 'Could you come over here and

read what it now says on top of Chef's "Good Luck, Polo Team" cake?'

I began to pull off the washing-up gloves. 'Actually,' Mum said quickly, 'I wouldn't bother taking those off. Come on, come over here and read it out.'

I shuffled towards them and leaned over the cake to see what all this fuss was about. When I saw what had happened, I burst out laughing. Mum and Chef shared a look of irritation.

'Well?' Mum prompted, as I clutched my stomach from laughing so hard. 'Read it out.'

I attempted to stifle the overwhelming giggles. 'Good lu–' I couldn't hold the laughter back. 'Good luck, p–' I couldn't breathe I was laughing too hard. 'Good luck, p–'. Tears were now streaming down my face.

'Felicity.'

My mum's fierce tone snapped me out of it immediately. I wiped my eyes before whispering what was now written across the cake.

'Louder, please,' Mum demanded. 'The chefs at the back didn't quite hear you.'

I took a deep breath. '"Good Luck, Poo Team".'

Sasha erupted into infectious giggles. Chef stared at her until she stopped but when he turned his back on her I could see her shoulders still shaking.

'It looks like you ate a rather important "L". It is lucky Chef has the time to redo it before he brings it up to the ballroom in a few minutes, after I've finished giving my speech to the guests.'

I looked down at my feet, my jaw aching from trying not to laugh.

'Right.' Mum clasped her hands together. 'Chef, if you could kindly put the finishing touches to the cake, I would like to have a serious word with my daughter.' She paused. 'For the second time today.'

Chef began to bark out orders and the kitchen burst into life again. Just before she rushed off to find some more chocolate buttons, Sasha grinned at me. At least I cheered someone up.

Mum waited until we were on our own before she spoke again.

'I would hate to extend those two weeks of being grounded to two months.'

'Two months?' I gasped. 'Mum, you ca—'

'Flick,' she interrupted sharply, 'I should have thought you might have learned by now that telling me what I can and cannot do does not help your case.'

I pursed my lips.

'Two strikes,' she said firmly. 'Strike three and it's two months. Understood?'

I nodded.

'Excellent. And you've gained yourself an extra hour down here.' She pointed to the sink behind me. 'Those pots won't wash themselves.'

FOUR

'Oh no.' Ella didn't look up from her phone. I may be reading into things but I'm not sure she was all that bothered about me missing her party.

'Yeah.' I nodded solemnly, having taken great pains to explain the situation in thorough detail. 'I did everything I could to change Mum's mind but you know what she can be like.'

'Sure.' Ella looked up at Grace, who was leaning on the locker next to her, fiddling with her split ends. 'Your brother and his friends are definitely coming, right?'

Ella and I had never actually spoken to Grace Dillon properly before this term but since Grace's brother in the year above suddenly got hot over the summer, Ella wanted her to hang out with us. According to Grace, her brother discovered the gym AND hair product at the same time. It also helped that he could play a guitar – at least, that's what Ella had swooned at when he played with his band in assembly at the beginning of term. Personally, I don't see the attraction. I would never date anyone who thinks it's acceptable to wear a sleeveless vest. Anyway, after his performance, Ella invited Grace to join us for a post-school smoothie and that was that; she became part of our elite group.

At first, I thought Grace was going to be this irritating suck-up as she actually did her homework and was top of the class for almost everything. But then one lunchtime, she made me laugh so hard that lemonade went right up my nose. After that, I quite liked her being around and she had this cute little habit of texting me about random stuff. She was obviously ecstatic to be allowed to hang out with us at school, which meant she was never in a bad mood, unlike Ella and her boring mood swings, which were becoming a lot more common these days.

Ella and I first bonded when our mums were both featured in this big newspaper article about leading businesswomen in the UK. Her mum is a co-founder of this online luxury furniture company, which apparently is a big deal, but obviously nowhere near as cool as being a hotelier. Anyway, Mum hosted a big exclusive party for all the women on the list at the Royale and Ella came with her mum. Ella and I both found the party super boring but the photographer took our picture and we were in the back pages of *Tatler* magazine. Ella showed everyone the picture and we instantly became the most popular girls in the year. After that it just made sense to keep hanging out together, especially when we both had important parents and such good dress sense.

Although, seriously, I wish she'd shut up about Oliver Dillon and his loser band.

'Absolutely,' Grace said enthusiastically. 'He'll be at your party. I told him to invite his friends and I know that Liam and Tom were both keen.'

'Well done.' Ella smiled smugly. 'It will be nice to have some mature boys there.'

'I wouldn't count on those two to bring up the maturity levels,' I added. 'Wasn't it Liam who drank a whole bottle of Worcester sauce for a dare?'

'Oh yeah.' Grace giggled. 'He threw up *everywhere*.'

'Oliver seems mature,' Ella said consideringly, taking her pocket mirror out and examining her eye make-up.

'Really is a shame I can't go,' I prompted.

'Has Oliver dated anyone at school?' Ella asked Grace, ignoring me completely. This was getting ridiculous. Couldn't she concentrate on anything else? Or me at least? She could show *some* emotion that I wouldn't be able to make it to her party.

'Why? Are you interested in him?' I said, cutting to the chase.

'Oh my God, *no*, I'm not interested. I was just asking.'

Ella fake-laughed before turning seriously to Grace again. 'Has he?'

Grace shook her head, before adding excitedly, 'He asked the same about you, though.'

'Really?' Ella snapped her mirror shut, her eyes widening.

'Yes, last night.'

'And what *exactly* did you say?'

Grace's cheeks turned pink under the pressure of Ella's fixed stare. 'Um ... I just said that you had that thing with Aidan ...'

'*Grace!*' Ella hissed. Grace cowered.

'Was that wrong?' she asked timidly.

'Why would you say that? Now he's going to think that I'm unavailable!'

Grace's face was now a bright red. 'N-no, I'm sure he doesn't think that. I can tell him that it's over with Aidan, I just wasn't certain.'

I couldn't help but feel sorry for Grace. She was very petite – the smallest girl in our year – so she looked even more vulnerable as Ella, who was one of the tallest, towered over her. Ella wasn't going to be forgiving. She never was. I would have to save the day.

'I think it's a good thing.'

Ella rounded on me. I could see Grace's shoulders

visibly relax as the heat was diverted on to someone else. 'What do you mean?'

I sighed at how clueless she was. 'If he wants to go out with you then he needs to make an effort. He can't just date you because he makes the decision to.'

Ella hesitated as she considered my point so I continued. 'You deserve the best, he has to prove that he is the best. Does that make sense?'

'I guess,' Ella said, her brow furrowed.

'Good work, Grace, you've probably made your brother keener than ever. Not that you're interested in him, right, Ella?'

'Right,' she said unconvincingly.

'But hey, he might just win you over at the party.'

Ella nodded. 'Yes. Yes, he might. Not that I'll be waiting around for him to make a move.'

'Duh, obviously not.' I paused. 'But just in case, how about you borrow my black leather mini that you love so much?'

'Really?'

I was satisfied to note that Ella turned to look at me properly for the first time since we'd started talking.

'Your new one?' she asked. 'But you haven't worn it yet.'

'That doesn't matter.' I forced a smile. 'It will look great on you.'

I hated lending anything to Ella. And not just because she never told anyone who complimented her on it that it was in fact MY stuff, but also because it meant I could never wear it again. Last year at a summer pool party, I wore a pair of really cute designer pink shorts that I had stupidly lent Ella the weekend before. And then Zoe, one of the girls in our year, asked me if *I* had borrowed them from *Ella*. It was MORTIFYING. Ella is my friend and everything, but *I* don't copy anyone. They copy *me*. I obviously had to go home straight away and change, and I threw the shorts in the bin. My brand-new leather skirt was now doomed to the same fate. But I guess it's like when celebrities go on those reality TV shows, eat bugs and dance and stuff, and come out with a new lingerie line and book deal. Sometimes sacrifices have to be made to get what you want.

'Great!' Ella whipped out her lip gloss, added another layer to her already way too shiny lips and snapped the lid back on. 'It really is such a shame that you can't come to the party, Flick. It won't be the same without you.'

Finally. The reaction I had been waiting for. Even if I did have to sacrifice my leather mini in the process. She flounced off towards her classroom and Grace breathed a sigh of relief.

'Thanks so much, Flick. I thought she was going to yell

at me then. You always know what to do. I wish I was more like you.'

I gave her arm a comforting pat.

THE DAILY POST

Skylar Touches Down in London!

By Nancy Rose

American teen pop star Skylar Chase has landed in the capital as she embarks on her first UK tour. The popular singer has been touring the world ever since her debut album exploded on to the charts, propelling her to number one for weeks, and beating the world record for longest album in the top spot. 'I'm excited to be here in London,' the eighteen year old told the Daily Post exclusively. 'I'll be here for a while to work on several projects, so I'm looking forward to seeing the sights as well as getting down to some hard work.' Rumour has it that while she's here in the UK, she will be staying at London's famous grande dame hotel, Hotel Royale. Only the best for this pop princess!

'Is it true? Is it true?'

Grace's sudden squealing jolted me from my phone. While the others had been sitting together, going on about Ella's party in the last few minutes of our lunch break, I had happily tucked myself away in a corner for some online shopping.

'Is what true?' I asked grumpily, quickly closing the page of leather skirts.

'This!' Grace shoved her phone, which was open on some celebrity gossip website, under my nose.

'Skylar Chase is in London,' I read. 'So?'

'Look at where she's staying!' Grace cried, her long black hair swishing into my face as she leaned over to point it out to me.

I read further down the piece and by the time I had scanned the paragraph, my desk was surrounded by an excitable, whispering crowd. This always happens when someone super famous stays at the hotel. Everyone at school becomes obsessed with following me around, asking for the celebrity's autograph or even sometimes just showing up at home. As my school is near to the hotel, this happens quite a lot. Matthew gets all grumpy when he has to shoo them away.

Ella pushed her way through the group at my desk before plonking herself importantly on the chair next to mine.

'Well?' she asked, tilting her head curiously.

'I'm not sure,' I answered honestly. 'It makes sense that she would be staying with us, though. Where else would she go?'

'Oh my God,' Grace squeaked. 'Imagine if you see her in the lobby!'

'Would she give you tickets to her tour?' Ella asked, shooting Grace a look of irritation as Grace practically hopped up and down on the spot.

'I'll probably get backstage passes.'

Grace's jaw dropped open. 'Do you think you'll get more than one backstage pass?'

'Grace, calm down,' Ella scolded, before rolling her eyes at me as Grace's face fell.

I smiled to myself, remembering a year ago when Ella had practically torn my arm off in her excitement of her favourite boy band staying at the hotel, begging me for tickets or a chance to bump into them in reception. Now she had her new minion to impress, she was better at keeping up appearances.

'If I get more than one pass, I'll be sure to let you know. I'll ask her if we hang out later.'

'Hang out?' Grace whispered, glancing nervously at Ella to confirm her tone and pitch were more acceptable.

'Of course.' I shrugged. 'Mum often asks me to hang

out with the VIP guests, you know, just to be polite.'

Grace put a hand on her heart as though to steady herself.

It wasn't a *complete* lie, either, Mum did sometimes force me to give up my evenings to hang out with guests, so that part was true. The more questionable part was the VIP side of things.

What actually happened was that any time Mum wanted to talk to a guest and they had a daughter or a son my age, she would insist I join them – for some reason, Mum seems to think that being a similar age means we will automatically get on. I've always had to stand there awkwardly and silently with some loser teenager while our parents talk rubbish until my promised hour is up and I can escape back to my room ASAP.

I never get to talk to anyone I've actually heard of, like famous actors or pop stars. Usually they have so much security it's impossible to get to them and I'm under strict instructions never to pester them or get in their way. The only time I really get to be in the same room as celebrities is the Hotel Royale Christmas Ball, which is my favourite night of the year and the biggest and best party in the world. Famous people and royal families from across the globe come to the hotel all dressed up in these amazing designer ballgowns, and they're always all over the front pages the next day. It's basically the Oscars but way better because there are no boring speeches and no one cries. Usually.

But other than the Christmas Ball, Mum always says that famous guests come to Hotel Royale to escape the fuss, and it's important to her that they feel they can relax in the hotel without feeling they're being watched or scrutinised. So there was no chance that Mum would let me go near someone as famous as Skylar Chase; I was never allowed to bother any celebrities.

But no one had to know that.

'You know, Flick –' Ella smiled – 'if you want to bring Skylar along to my party next week, I wouldn't mind.'

Gasps rippled through our audience.

'That is,' she continued, 'if you manage to persuade your mum to let you come.'

'I'll see what I can do.'

Everyone around us burst into chatter and Ella looked extremely pleased with herself, no doubt dying inside at the idea of Skylar Chase attending HER party. Obviously, it was never going to happen but I couldn't shoot her down straight away, not with the whole class watching.

Hey Grace

Hey Flick! Wassup?

Not to be weird but . . . are you
following me home?

What?! Course not!

OK. It's only . . . I can see you

What do you mean? I'm on my way home.
Which is the opposite direction to the hotel

I can see you behind that lamp post

What lamp post?

The one you're hiding behind

That must be someone else

I just saw you type that text

Must be someone else texting while
we're texting too. Weird coincidence!

I can literally see you. Right there behind that lamp post

Are you sure you're not following me? No offence, but that's kind of creepy

I told you that if I see Skylar Chase, I'll call you immediately, OK? And when I'm not grounded any more, you can come to the hotel after school

THANK YOU!

No worries. You can leave the lamp post now and go home

I totally wasn't following you
That would be weird

Right

I had to come this way to check out . . . this lamp post

> **Sure. That makes sense**

> It's a historical gem

> **Go home Grace**

When I got home, I couldn't help but get a teeny bit excited that Skylar Chase might be there. There were LOADS of photographers and reporters lurking around the entrance, getting in the way and ignoring the dirty looks from the doormen, who were attempting to welcome guests. I'm not supposed to talk to journalists, especially not about guests staying at the hotel, and thanks to Mum not letting me do any self-promotion they're never interested in taking *my* picture. But some of the reporters know who I am and they gave me a friendly nod as I went round the revolving doors into reception.

What if I actually did bump into her? I looked about for any sign that the biggest pop star on the planet was staying in the hotel but everything looked exactly as it always did: Matthew was speaking on the phone behind the reception desk, a porter tipped his hat at me as I walked past, and guests wandered by on their way to their bedroom or the tearoom. The only thing that was different was that the extravagant flower arrangements around the lobby had been changed from pink flowers to purple ones.

'Ah, Flick, I've been waiting for you.'

I grimaced as Audrey came down the stairs. Before this whole Skylar-Chase thing distracted me, I'd been planning on racing straight to my room when I got home, thus avoiding any run-ins with Audrey or Matthew. My dawdling had cost me.

'I'm impressed. I thought you might run straight to your room and try to avoid me,' she admitted.

'Why would you think that?'

'Oh, I don't know. Maybe because on any other occasion that your mother has asked you to help someone in the hotel, you've rushed to your room, locked the door and pretended to be asleep.'

'Did you want something, or were you just looking for me to tell me off?' I huffed.

'I need your help with a small task in the restaurant.'

'Great, OK, but I have to go and walk Fritz and then I'll be with you.'

'I thought you might say that, which is why I asked Jamie to take Fritz out about fifteen minutes ago. I'm sure Fritz is having a marvellous time in the park right now. So, to the restaurant.' She smiled, ushering me towards it.

'You can help set up for the first dinner sitting.'

I was surprised by how mild the job allocation was – how hard can it be to set out a few knives and forks? – but I groaned loudly for effect so she wouldn't think I was getting away with it.

'Ah, Timothy.' Audrey beckoned over one of the waiters folding napkins. I recognised him from the other day when he annoyingly interrupted my conversation with Mum about the selfie stick. 'Flick will be assisting you for the next hour. Is it OK if I leave her in your charge?'

'Absolutely,' he said cheerily. 'Welcome to the team, Flick.'

I did my best unimpressed face.

'I'll let you get started then,' Audrey said, clapping her hands together before sauntering back to reception.

Timothy gestured for me to follow him to a trolley on which there was a large, shiny silver tray. Piled up on it was what looked like a hundred different pieces of cutlery.

'Terrifying, isn't it?' He chuckled. 'Don't worry, you'll soon get the hang of it. I'll run through what each knife and fork is for, and so on and so forth, and then you can watch me do some settings before having a go yourself. Does that sound like a plan?'

I pursed my lips together.

'Er . . . great,' he said nervously. 'Let's begin with the

forks.' He selected several forks from the tray and held them up. 'This is a fish fork, this one is a dinner fork and this one is a salad fork. Then you've got this little mite, the cocktail fork.' He chuckled but stopped at my expression, placing the forks down quickly. 'Now, the knives. This one is a –'

'Timothy!'

Another waiter walked briskly towards us. 'Apologies for interrupting, Miss Royale. Timothy, you're needed briefly in the kitchen.'

'Right, well, Flick, you just wait here a minute, I'll be back in a tick. And then we'll go through the knives.'

'Can't wait.' I rolled my eyes and sat down.

Timothy and the other waiter shared a look before they hurried away. I picked up one of the forks and examined the patterns engraved into it, wondering why we didn't have such fancy cutlery in our apartment. Mum is so stingy.

Throwing the fork on the top of the cutlery pile with a loud clang, I looked impatiently about me at the vast, empty dining room. I eyed up the door in the far corner which led to the piano room, a much smaller event space for musical performances – Cal and I used it to spy on dinner guests when we were little until we got told off for getting in the way. Timothy was nowhere to be seen and, no doubt, he would be kept busy for a while in the kitchen. *Technically*, I'd done what I'd been told to do and the person in charge of me was shirking his duties. Smugly, I rushed over to the door. I hesitated when I heard Timothy's voice coming down the corridor towards the restaurant. It was now or never. I pushed the door, slipped through and closed it behind me quickly, leaning back and breathing a sigh of relief. No more fish-fork lectures for me.

'Mwahahaha,' I whispered gleefully to myself, revelling in the silence of the piano room and my cunning escape. It would be easy to slip up to my room from here using the back stairs without being seen by Audrey and Matthew who are always front of house. No one would catch me here.

'Hi.'

I yelped as someone stood up from the stool behind the grand piano.

My breath caught in my throat as I saw who it was.

Skylar Chase.

FIVE

'Sorry, I didn't mean to scare you.'

For a few moments I just stared at her, taking in the fact that Skylar Chase, the most famous pop star in the world, was standing in front of me and had just heard me say 'mwahahaha' to myself for no apparent reason.

It wasn't exactly the introduction I'd hoped for.

'No, don't worry about it,' I said eventually, pulling myself together. 'Sorry, I didn't realise you were in here.'

'I was just . . .' She gestured to the piano as she came forwards to lean on its side.

I nodded. 'Cool. Well, I'll get out of your way.'

'I recognise you,' she said curiously. 'Aren't you . . . Felicity Royale?'

I gaped at her. 'You . . . *you* know who *I* am?'

'I met your mom earlier, she showed me a picture of you.'

'Oh no.' I winced. 'I'm sorry. Was she really embarrassing?'

She laughed. 'No! No, she was very welcoming. It was nice to meet her.'

'Yeah, well she's not exactly up to date with the charts or anything,' I explained as she giggled. 'Don't be insulted if she talks about music from hundreds of years ago.'

'I'll keep that in mind.' She smiled, showing her perfect set of pearly white teeth.

This may sound stupid, but you know there's that saying about how some people just have 'star quality'? Well, Skylar Chase has it. Whatever it is. Her aura or something. It just radiates out, a sort of comfortableness in her own skin.

And the way she looked too. I was still in my school uniform, whereas she was wearing a white blouse, skinny black jeans, black heeled boots, and a black trilby hat which was resting perfectly on the top of her curly brown hair. She really did look every inch a pop star.

Despite the fact that I had just interrupted an international musician rehearsing her songs so should probably leave her to it, something about the way she leaned on the piano watching me made me feel like she wanted to keep talking.

'Shouldn't a famous pop star have an entourage or something?'

She rolled her eyes. 'I actually do have a pretty big

team staying here but I wanted to get away for a bit.'

'Do they tell you how great you are the whole time?'

'Not nearly enough.' She grinned. 'What was with the cackle?'

'Huh?'

'The cackle you did when you came into the room.'

'I didn't do a cackle.'

'You did. You went, "Mwahahaha." Like an evil villain laugh.'

'No, I didn't.'

'You definitely did. It wasn't a very good one, but it was one nonetheless.'

'What do you mean it wasn't very good?'

'There was no power in it; you didn't use your diaphragm. Like this.' She threw me a mischievous smile before flinging her head back and really going for it. 'MWAHAHAHA!'

'Wow.' I laughed, trying to ignore how surreal this all was and act as though I chat to famous pop stars all the time. 'Much better than mine.'

'Aha! Then you do admit you did it!'

'Fine, I admit there was a slight cackle.'

'So, then.' She folded her arms triumphantly. 'Why?'

I hesitated. 'Long story short, I got in a bit of trouble recently so Mum grounded me and is making me help out around the hotel.'

'If you're grounded, doesn't that mean you can't leave your house?' she asked, with furrowed eyebrows.

'Right. I'm stuck here.'

'Wait a second.' She looked at me in disbelief. 'You *live* here?'

I nodded.

'In the hotel? In Hotel Royale?'

'I know, it's weird.'

'Weird?' Her expression broke into a wide grin. 'It's SO COOL!'

'I guess it has its moments.'

'You must order room service the whole time. I would.'

'Mum doesn't let me,' I admitted, pleased to have someone else on my wavelength. 'She likes to keep everything as normal as possible. Our flat has a kitchen and everything, so I'm not allowed to use any of the hotel perks.'

'You have a flat in the hotel?'

'Yeah, it takes up most of the fifteenth floor.'

She shook her head in amazement. 'So, being grounded in your terms means you get to hang out in the most amazing hotel in the city?'

'That's one way of looking at it.' I shrugged. 'But it's just home to me.'

'And part of your punishment is helping out? Doesn't sound like much of a punishment. Must be cool to see how it all works.'

'Wait until you see the number of forks there are.' I sighed. 'Your turn.'

'My turn what?' she asked, baffled.

'I told you why I did the evil cackle, now you tell me why you're on your own hiding out in a piano room when you've only just arrived in London.'

It was her turn to sigh. 'Sometimes all the photographers, and the fans, and being told exactly where to be and when, with no time to myself . . . I just haven't stopped.' She bit her lip. 'Sounds selfish, doesn't it?'

I shook my head. 'Not really. I can see why sometimes you'd want to sneak away and have a breather from it all.'

'Right.' She nodded slowly. 'I could have just played the piano in my room, I guess, but I didn't want to kick my team out when they're so busy sorting the schedule. I needed a bit of space and your mom mentioned you had a piano room so I thought I'd sneak out for a bit. Playing the piano is very calming. I feel much better now.'

'Then you should sneak out more often.'

She smiled and then held out her hand. 'I'm Sky, by the way.'

'I know. And it's Flick, rather than Felicity,' I said, stepping forwards to shake it.

'It's really nice to meet you. Hey, do you –'

Suddenly the main door swung open and my mum marched in, followed closely by Audrey and a worried-looking Timothy.

'Flick, I can't believe . . . Oh.' Mum came to a halt when she saw who I was talking to. 'Miss Chase.'

'Hi, Christine.' Skylar gave her a cheery wave.

'I'm so sorry,' she said quickly. 'I can't believe my daughter has been disturbing you when you've obviously been trying to rehearse. She was meant to be helping Timothy with . . . Well, never mind. Flick, I thought I made myself clear, you were –'

'Actually,' Skylar interrupted, 'this is all my fault.'

'It is?' Mum said.

'It is?' I squeaked.

'Yes, of course,' she said breezily. 'You see, I've been writing a new song and I was desperate to show it to someone. I couldn't tell if it was any good and I was going to call up to the room and see if anyone could come down, but I'm sure you understand, Christine, my team are extremely busy.'

'I . . . I can imagine,' Mum replied, looking from Skylar to me very suspiciously.

'I didn't want to disturb them so I popped my head through this door here and I saw Flick placing the . . . forks.' She turned to me. 'Right?'

'That's right.' I nodded vigorously. 'The fish fork, the dinner fork, the salad fork and the cocktail fork.'

Mum and Audrey looked surprised. Behind them, Timothy gave me a very proud thumbs up.

'I asked her if she wouldn't mind listening to my song and she came through to offer her criticism. She took a lot of persuading, because she was really focused on the . . . um . . . silverware, but I begged her to help. It was very kind of her to risk getting in trouble for me.'

'Anything for a guest. Right, Mum?' I smiled sweetly.

'So, as you can see –' Skylar sighed heavily – 'it was all my fault and I'm sorry for causing trouble.'

'No need to say sorry,' Mum said quickly. 'I hope we didn't interrupt.'

'It's a good thing you did, actually –' Skylar checked her sparkly diamond watch – 'I better go back before my tour manager loses her mind.'

She strode past the three of them to the door and, pulling it towards her, she stopped to look back at me. 'See you around, Flick.' She grinned.

And with that she swanned out of the room, all of us watching her go.

What's she like then?

Who is this? I don't have this number saved

Ouch. That hurt. No, wait. I don't care. What's Skylar Chase like?

WHO IS THIS?

Caps lock, eh? Must be getting angry

?!?!?!?!?!

When's your vlog going to be up and running? I need to subscribe. But WAIT! How can you possibly do anything without your selfie stick?! PRINCE GUSTAV, YOU ROGUE! CALL THE NATIONAL GUARD! ALERT THE QUEEN! TELL MI6 TO SEND THEIR BEST AGENT!

Cal. I should have known it was you

From my wit and charm?

From how annoying you are. What do you want? How did you get this number?

Audrey gave it to me. She said you and Skylar were hanging out

What's it to you?

No need to get so touchy

Look, I'm very busy. In answer to your question, Skylar is very nice. OK? Leave me alone now

Busy watching YouTube videos of puppies barking at themselves in the mirror?

ARE YOU IN MY FLAT? EW!

Chill out, Audrey said you were obsessed with those stupid videos. It was a lucky guess

Audrey needs to stop talking about me to you. It's invasion of privacy.

68

I told you what Skylar was like. So leave me alone

Fine. I was actually texting you to let you know that Chef has saved a plate for you from dinner but I'll let him know that you don't want it. I was just asking you about Skylar Chase to be polite

Wait, what?? NO don't tell him that!

Sorry. Too late. I just threw it away

You are such a moron

SIX

I didn't tell anyone at school about Skylar Chase.

I know, weird, right? Usually if I meet anyone remotely famous I phone Ella straight away and know it will be all over school by the next morning, but it just felt different with Skylar. I couldn't put my finger on it. It's not like I didn't get the chance to tell anyone, either – Grace ambushed me the moment I stepped on to school property, asking me a hundred questions all at once about whether she was actually staying there, if I'd spoken to her and whether or not it's true she had a fling with Justin Bieber. Without even thinking, I lied and said I hadn't seen her, before changing the subject.

Grace looked disappointed but cheered up at lunch when she excitedly announced that the *Daily Post* had confirmed Skylar Chase was staying at Hotel Royale. She'd been spotted leaving the hotel with a huge entourage that morning. Everyone turned to wait for my reaction but I just shrugged, saying I'd let them know if I saw her. Satisfied with my answer, Ella turned the discussion to who was wearing what to her party and which boys were going to be there, a conversation that continued at my locker as I got my books out for the last lessons of the day.

'So, definitely the green top over the pink?' she asked for the fifth time that day.

'Yes,' I replied irritably.

'Tights or no tights?'

'Uh-uh,' I said automatically, struggling to find my maths book in the bomb site that was my locker.

'I guess it depends on the shoes I'm wearing.' She sighed heavily, as though dealing with a world catastrophe. 'And I don't know whether to curl my hair or leave it straight. Maybe I'll get a blow-dry. There's so much to think about.'

'Sure,' I answered, finally tugging out my maths book.

It sent everything else in my locker flying out with it, scattering books and loose paper all over the floor. I groaned and crouched down to start picking it all up when I noticed someone else bend down next to me to help. Oliver, Grace's brother, gathered together the loose sheets and handed them to me.

'Thanks,' I said gratefully, standing up and awkwardly trying to balance everything in my arms.

'That's OK.' He laughed, immediately catching a

book falling from my grip. 'You got it all?'

'Yep.' I shoved everything back into my locker, taking the final book from him, throwing it on the top of the pile and closing the locker door quickly.

'You do know that it will all fall out again as soon as you open your locker door,' he commented.

'I know,' I grumbled. 'I need a new locker. This one's WAY too small. I did formally request they get bigger lockers last term but they just ignored me. This school is so mean. If I get flattened by one of these books falling on top of me, I will be able to sue.'

Oliver laughed as though I'd told a hilarious joke.

Quite frankly I see nothing funny about this school's clear lack of concern for their students' well-being but whatever, he clearly has a weird sense of humour.

Since Oliver had come over, Ella had been too busy vying for his attention to help me pick anything up. She fidgeted with the hem of her skirt and twirled a lock of her glossy brown hair.

'That was kind of you, Oliver,' she said in a sickly sweet voice. 'Flick's locker has always been a disaster. She's so lazy.'

I did a double take at her face as I noticed her lips were much shinier than they had been a moment before. She must have added a slick of lip gloss as soon as Oliver bent down to help me pick everything up.

'I'm looking forward to your party next week, Ella.' Oliver smiled, showing off his prominent cheekbones.

Ella giggled stupidly. 'It's going to be *so* fun.'

'You going, Flick?' he asked, his eyes flashing towards me.

'She's grounded,' Ella replied flippantly.

'What did you do to get grounded?'

'I hope you've invited all your friends,' Ella interrupted, before I could answer. 'I've got a proper DJ and a photo booth.'

'Sounds cool. Well, I better get going. See you around.'

Ella watched him stroll down the corridor and join his friends who were waiting for him. When he turned the corner, Ella leaned back against the locker. 'Did you see his eyes?' she said, still in a daze. 'So dark and mysterious – and he has such good eyelashes. They're so long, aren't they?'

'I didn't notice.'

'They are amazing. Are you sure he'd like the green top? Not that I care.'

'Why don't you ask Grace?'

'That's a good idea.'

She swanned off and I sighed with relief. I don't think I could have faced the last five minutes of lunch break listening to her drone on about Oliver Dillon's long eyelashes. I watched her pootle down to where Grace was glued to her phone – no doubt reading the latest about Skylar Chase – and then I turned to slam straight into Cal Weston.

'Watch where you're going!' I snarled.

'You walked into *me*,' he huffed. I moved to step around him but he grabbed my arm.

'Hey,' he said, so quietly I could barely hear him, 'how come you're not telling anyone about your run-in with Skylar Chase?'

'None of your business,' I snapped. 'Don't say anything, OK?'

He held up his hands. 'I wouldn't dare.'

'Good.'

'I'm just surprised you're not basking in the glory of your new-found friend.'

'Are you this annoying with everyone or do you just save it all up for me?'

'I like to keep the top of my game just for you.' He grinned. 'Does that make you feel special?'

'Urgh, you are so weird.' I looked around quickly to make sure no one was watching and lowered my voice. 'Seriously, I don't want to tell anyone about talking to Skylar. Whatever you do, don't tell Grace Dillon.'

'What's wrong with Grace Dillon?' he asked, craning over me to watch her nodding vigorously at whatever Ella was saying. 'I thought she was all right. Well, she was, until she started tagging along with you and Her Royal Highness over there.'

'Just don't say anything, OK?'

'Fine, your secret is safe with me. It just seems –' he paused – 'unlike you.'

'Is that a compliment?'

'If you want it to be.'

I rolled my eyes. 'I can't explain it. Skylar was . . . normal. I don't know, it seems wrong to blurt about it to everyone. I can't explain,' I repeated.

Cal nodded, watching me closely. 'No need to.' He shrugged and then ended the conversation by sauntering off down the corridor.

I glared at his back as he walked off. I don't know why he has to be so cryptic all the time, as though he knows something that no one else does. Whatever. I had more important things to think about than Cal Weston. Like, how I was going to escape tonight's boring hotel chore. Please, please don't let it be anything to do with Matthew and the hotel booking system.

PLEASE.

'And that leads you on to the main booking system,' Matthew announced proudly, clicking the mouse and loading what looked like the most boring spreadsheet of all time. 'Easy, eh? Just one click. I tell you, technology is a marvellous thing.'

I tried and failed to seem enthused. Matthew sighed.

'Is any of this going through into that brain of yours?' He reached for one of the many dust cloths he kept next to the branded fountain pens and began to polish away a barely noticeable smear on the shiny desk.

'Honestly, Matthew? No.' I yawned, leaning back in my chair.

'I thought as much. Always been a fan of your honesty, though.' He smiled, winking at me. I stood up briefly to see over the reception desk and check on Fritz, who was sitting in his armchair as usual, greeting guests. At that moment, he was having his belly rubbed by a duchess, who was speaking to him in a baby voice, so I left him to it and sat back down.

'How did it go with Prince Gustav?' Matthew asked.

I shrugged. 'Fine. He was nice about it. I gave him some selfie-stick tips and by the end he was practically begging me to stay to teach him more. I wish he'd tell Mum that I've been punished enough.'

'Do you think you have?'

'Are you kidding? I've had to do a hundred boring things.'

He raised his eyebrows.

'Mum's being so harsh.'

'Can you blame her? She's under a lot of stress, what with the Christmas Ball approaching.'

I snorted. 'Like she has much to do with that. Audrey organises the whole thing.'

'Oh, I wouldn't be so sure.' Matthew folded the dust cloth and placed it neatly back next to the fountain pens. 'Audrey does a huge amount, of course, but your mother heads up the entire operation. Not to mention how much she does to run this place.'

'She doesn't have to take her stress out on me.'

'She just wants it all to go smoothly. And this time of year there's always plenty to do – the Christmas Ball means a lot to her.'

'Duh, it's the best night ever. And she gets to flirt with George Clooney.' I rolled my eyes.

Matthew shook his head. 'It's not that. Maybe you should ask her sometime.'

'Whatever, she's been *totally* unfair to me. I apologised to Prince Gustav so I don't understand why I'm still being punished,' I huffed.

He laughed and shook his finger at me. 'That stubborn expression of yours reminds me of the time when I caught you swapping the keys around so all the guests got the wrong key to their room. Do you remember?'

'That was Cal's idea,' I lied. 'But I was the one who got in trouble.'

'I find that hard to believe.' He smiled, his eyes twinkling. 'You were the brains behind all your operations.'

'I always took the fall for Cal, if that's what you mean.'

'Trust me, he didn't get away with anything. I may be a jolly worker, but make no mistake, I'm a very strict father.' He straightened up as a guest approached the desk, greeting them like they were an old friend whom he hadn't seen in ages.

While I waited for him to finish, the phone began to ring next to me. All the phones at reception were gold-plated vintage ones, with a rotary dial and everything, and they had that old-fashioned trill ring. They totally suited the decor.

I watched it ring and I could see Matthew glancing at it out the corner of his eye but the guest was in full flow, telling him all about his trip to the zoo and, as the politest man of all time, Matthew wouldn't dream of breaking away mid-conversation. The phone continued to ring. I just stared at it at first but then it started to bug me so

I craned my neck over the desk to see if any porters were nearby, but they were all busy. I put my hands over my ears grumpily until FINALLY Audrey appeared and snatched it up. She did a lot of 'uh-uh's and 'mm's and then went, 'of course, straight away,' before neatly placing the receiver down.

'You took long enough,' I said, as she turned to face me with her hand on her hip. 'Is there any way of turning down the volume on that thing?'

'You know that is the internal line, right? I've told you several times before.'

'Yeah. So?'

'So,' she said through gritted teeth, 'you could have picked up, as it was a guest in the hotel and not someone phoning to make a booking.'

'I don't work here, Audrey. You can't expect me to just jump in when you're understaffed. This isn't the industrial revolution; child labour isn't fashionable any more.'

Audrey took a deep breath. I had made a valid point and she knew it. I can't answer the phones. It's not my fault I happen to live here.

'I suppose you're right,' she said, her tone oddly flat. 'I shouldn't expect that of you.'

'Apology accepted.'

'For reasons I can't possibly imagine, Skylar Chase

has requested your presence in her suite.'

I stared at her. 'W-what? Are you sure?'

'Quite sure. That was her on the phone. She wants Flick Royale to go straight to her room if she is home from school and if she is not busy.'

'Why?'

'She didn't say.'

'And you're certain she asked for me?'

'Yes.'

'Seriously?'

'Flick.' Audrey began tapping her shoe impatiently. 'I am certain that Skylar Chase requests your company this very moment. She's in Room 108. It goes without saying that you do not pass on that information. Now, I suggest you get up there pronto. Don't worry about Fritz, I'll have someone bring him upstairs when he's ready.' She clicked her fingers at me. 'Come on, look lively.'

I quickly stood up and hurried out from reception towards the lift, feeling completely shocked. My heartbeat was out of control as I arrived at her floor and stood stone still outside Room 108. I lifted my hand to knock on her door and froze, swallowing a lump in my throat. What could she possibly want?

The door swung open before I'd knocked, my hand still raised in preparation. Skylar Chase stood in front of me, wearing the hotel's white fluffy dressing gown and matching slippers.

'How long were you going to stand out there?' she said.

'Uhhh,' I replied intelligently.

'Come in!' she ushered, shutting the door behind me as I shuffled forwards. 'I need your help.'

She rushed off into the bedroom, leaving me standing awkwardly by the door. Her suite was the biggest and most beautiful in the hotel. It had a gigantic living room, a bedroom with a four-poster bed, a sparkling bathroom complete with hot tub, and a dressing room. The living room was filled with fresh bouquets of red roses – presumably her favourite flowers – and there was a grand piano at the far end of the room underneath a large window, which had an amazing view, looking out across London. The purple velvet curtains were currently closed so the room was bathed in the bright light of the chandeliers.

I had once asked Mum why our flat didn't look anything like this and she'd just brushed me off, telling me that no one would actually like to live in a place this grand.

To this day I don't know what she's talking about. Bring on the chandeliers.

'Why are you just standing there?' Skylar said, popping her head round the bedroom door. 'Come through.'

'Are you sure it was me you wanted?' I asked, following her instruction and making my way into her bedroom.

'Of course.' She was standing next to her bed, on which there were piles and piles of clothes. 'It's an emergency.'

'What's the problem? Because, if it's something with the room, I'm not really the right person to –'

'So, here's the thing,' she interrupted, 'I gave my team the evening off. They've been working really hard so I insisted on it and they all got really excited and they've gone sightseeing or something. And I've got this dinner to go to with some friends tonight and normally my stylist or PA would help me pick out what to wear but I don't want to ring them and disturb them from looking round that big tower thing. What's it called?'

'The Tower of London?'

'Yeah. Where all the heads were chopped off.' She wrinkled her nose. 'I couldn't think of anyone to call in London. Then I thought of you.'

'Me?'

'Yes, you. I remembered that you said you were grounded so I figured you'd be somewhere in the hotel this evening and probably looking for another escape from whatever you were doing.'

I broke into a grin. 'You were spot on.'

'Great!' She smiled back. 'Will you help?'

'Sure.' I pulled out the chair from the dressing table and sat down.

'I just need someone to make sure I don't look terrible. You won't believe how nasty the Internet can be when you get it wrong.' She pointed at the huge pile of clothes on the bed. 'These are my favourite options.'

'Right, so just a small task then.'

'Let's start with this pink dress,' she suggested, snatching it up and scurrying into her bathroom. I relaxed back into the chair and smiled to myself. It was easy to forget that you were with the most famous pop star in the world when you were hanging out with Skylar Chase. The way she talked and acted – it was just like being with a friend.

A very glamorous, insanely cool friend.

'OK, here's the first one.' She emerged from the bathroom and did a twirl. 'What do you think?'

I burst out laughing. 'It's a big fat no from the judges.'

'Why? I quite liked this one!'

'You won't when you see how it looks in this lighting.'

She went to admire herself in the full-length mirror and gasped. 'It's completely see-through!'

'It would certainly make the headlines,' I pointed out and we both erupted into giggles.

'On to the next one!'

After going through half of the pile, we finally decided on a beautiful red mini dress with sparkling silver shoes.

'You look amazing.' I nodded. My eyes widened as she opened a trunk filled to the brim with handbags, carefully selecting a silver clutch to finish the look. 'Where's your dinner then?'

'It's here in the hotel,' she said, putting on some diamond earrings while I moved to sit on the floor and dig through her treasure trove of handbags.

'You want to come?' she said suddenly.

I dropped the bag I had been fiddling with. 'What?'

'It's a dinner with some friends of mine, very casual.'

'Yeah, it seems very casual.' I laughed, nodding at the diamond bracelet she was putting on.

'I mean it. You should come.'

'I . . . I can't. I don't know anyone and I have nothing to wear and –'

'I think we could find you something.' She pointed at the bed of clothes. 'I get sent stuff in all kinds of sizes. We could find something small enough to fit.'

'You don't want me tagging along.'

'I've asked you, haven't I?'

I was stunned into silence. I couldn't believe that Skylar Chase was asking me to dinner with her *friends*.

'Come on!' She grinned. 'Don't make me beg. Plus, it's not technically breaking your mom's rules as you won't be leaving the hotel. So?'

I continued to stare at her, completely baffled at what was happening. 'If you're sure . . .'

'Great!' She shook off her heels and rushed over to the bed. 'I think I have the perfect thing in here that will look amazing with your beautiful red hair,' she announced, clothes flying across the room as she made her way through the pile. 'Wait until they find out I'm bringing you, Flick Royale of Hotel Royale!'

I sat in a daze. I had a feeling that she thought I was a bit more important than I was.

And there was nothing wrong with just going along with it, was there?

I need my lip gloss back

I haven't got your lip gloss, Ella. You were using it today

Not that one. My berry one. I lent it to you weeks ago

Yeah and I gave it right back. I just wanted to see if it really smelled like berries. I didn't actually use it

If you've lost it, you should buy me a new one. It will go perfectly with the green top

I've got to go, talk later

I stole Ella's lip gloss

The one she's looking for? Grace, you need to give it back, she thinks I have it

I know, she texted me saying you were refusing to give it back. Then I realised what had happened. I can't give it back. I donated it to Battersea Dogs Home

You donated a LIP GLOSS to Battersea Dogs Home?! Grace, do you know what Battersea Dogs Home is??

It was by accident. I donated them my cardigan and it was in the pocket

You donated a CARDIGAN? Grace, it's a DOGS HOME

Dogs get cold too

You're going to have to buy her a new one. She'll get really angry. You know what she's like

Yeah. The other day she yelled at me because I bought a polka dot pencil case and she has a polka dot pencil case. I had to return it

Grace, I've gotta go. I'm on my way to . . . well, an important dinner

Your life is so amazing. You get to spend evenings going to posh dinners. I, meanwhile, have to spend the evening cleaning out my tortoise hutch

You have a tortoise??

I never told you about Bruce?
He was a birthday present a couple of
years ago from my uncle who owns a
tortoise shelter in New Zealand. He's
getting really big now. The other day
he ate my eyelash curler thinking it was a leaf

How can you mistake an
eyelash curler for a LEAF?

I dunno. Ask Bruce

Grace. You are so weird.
But you really make me laugh

Thanks! Have a good night. Bruce
says "WASSUP!" (joking. Tortoises
can't talk. I made that up)

Thanks for clarifying. Night, Grace x

Up until two years ago when I stopped trying, I was the lead in all the school plays. And obviously now I wouldn't be seen dead auditioning for whatever lame production my school puts on next but, I have to admit, being in the spotlight was quite a lot of fun, and sometimes I do consider returning to the stage, but then I realise that doing so would mean spending a LOT of time with the drama club and, no offence to them, but they are *exhausting*.

For example, once I saw Hannah, the Queen Bee of the drama department, sitting on her own at a party, so I selflessly ditched my friends to go over to her so she wouldn't feel like such a loner, but she was utterly ungrateful about the whole thing. All I was saying was how I thought the play she had just been in was nice, but the ending was completely predictable and it would have been really cool if they'd mixed it up a bit more and had the fairy queen do something totally dramatic, like kill that boring fairy king, who was topless and everything, but such a creep. She looked at me in disgust and went all narkily, 'Sorry, but some of us don't think Shakespeare's works need "mixing up",' and then just got up and walked away.

Some people have no manners. And so, for that and several other reasons, I left my theatre career behind and believed that because of Mum's unnecessarily strict vlogging rules, I had stepped out of the spotlight for good.

That is, until I went for dinner with Skylar Chase.

Because that is what it's like when you walk around somewhere with her, it's like being onstage all the time, followed by a constant spotlight. And that's just walking from her suite to the dining room downstairs, it's not even leaving the hotel and going out into the real world. People stared at us as we walked down the corridor, then they stared at us in the lift, and then they stared at us walking from the lift and into the restaurant. And it felt GREAT. In fact, the only time we weren't being stared at was when I persuaded Skylar to hide with me behind one of the massive vases near reception for a few minutes on our way to the restaurant because Audrey was prowling about the lobby.

'Is it always like this?' I asked, as we reached the dining room and pretended not to notice all the turning heads.

'Yes.' Skylar nodded wearily.

'It's so much fun.' I smiled, lovingly stroking the clutch bag she had lent me.

'You think?' Skylar shook her head. 'It's like being on a permanent catwalk.'

'You say that like it's a bad thing.'

She looked at me curiously. 'You don't think you'd get bored of it?'

'Of being admired and adored?' I flashed her a smile. 'Oh, I think I could handle it.'

She laughed as Timothy came hurrying over to us, clutching some menus in his hands. He did a double take at me, possibly because when I usually come down to the restaurant I'm accompanied by a sausage dog in a tailored suit, not a world-famous pop star. Or it might have been down to my hair – Skylar had plaited it into a pretty braid across the top of my head like a halo and clipped a blue flower into it, matching the blue pleated skirt she'd chosen for me.

'Miss Chase, we have your table ready and your guests have arrived,' he began, before glancing at me. 'And will Miss Royale be joining the party?'

'She will.' Skylar beamed at me.

'No trouble at all. I'll sort out another setting.'

As he scampered away to huddle together with the

other waiters and rearrange the settings, a boy approached us with his arms outstretched towards Skylar.

'You finally made it to the best city in the world.' He grinned, as she squealed and embraced him. 'Took you long enough.'

I recognised him straight away: Ethan Duke, the YouTuber. Grace would have passed out on the spot. We'd spent hours at school watching his vlogs in lunch breaks. According to the 'About Me' section on his website, which Grace had memorised word for word, the story went that he happened to grow up next door to, and become best friends with, the son of a director, who let him tag along to a load of movie sets. Ethan started asking the super famous actors if they'd let him interview them for his YouTube channel during their filming breaks, and before long he had millions of followers and a queue of celebrities wanting to appear in one of his vlogs. Sometimes they were interviews, sometimes they were dares and sometimes he and a celebrity would team up to play a big prank on another celebrity.

He also happened to be the hottest person on the planet. In person he was more good-looking than in his videos, which I'd thought impossible. His sleek brown hair swept perfectly across his forehead, just above the thick eyebrows that framed his hazel-coloured eyes and he had these really full lips. I could not stop staring at his perfectly square jaw. How was anything that chiselled? I had to stop staring at it.

Look away from the jaw, look away from the jaw, look away from the jaw . . .

'Flick, this is Ethan.'

I was so deep in my examination of his angelic face, that when Skylar addressed me, I wasn't ready to form words.

'Jaw!'

Oh my God.

Skylar blinked at me. 'Huh?'

'I mean, four!' I said quickly, trying to save the situation. 'Four . . . forks. That's how many forks there will be. Four.'

'Flick, what are you talking about?'

'The number of forks at a place setting. I was just . . . uh . . . checking that everything was in order. Timothy!' I croaked, waiting for him to sidle up to me. 'Are there four forks at each place? As usual?'

'Yes . . .' he replied slowly, as though expecting it to be a trick question.

'Excellent,' I said, patting him on the arm awkwardly. 'Well done. You can go now.'

'Thank you, Miss Royale.' He backed away, his eyebrows knitted in confusion.

'Royale?' Ethan repeated in wonder. 'As in, Hotel Royale?'

CHANGE IN CONVERSATION = VERY GOOD RIGHT NOW.

'Yes.' I nodded, enthusiastically. 'You know it?'

'Hotel Royale? Yes. We're in it.'

CHANGE IN CONVERSATION = DID NOT GO SO WELL.

'Right, of course. Sorry, I drank a lot of coffee today.' I laughed nervously.

'I know the feeling. Nice to meet you, Flick, I'm Ethan.'

Skylar, still watching me strangely, gestured towards another guy and a girl who had come over while I had been yabbering about forks.

'This is Carly, my drummer, and you might recognise Jacob. He's a model.'

I thought it wise not to say anything this time, and nodded hello to both of them. We were guided across the room by Timothy, receiving plenty of stares and whispers around the room in the process. I made the conscious decision to try to sit away from Ethan (as apparently his jaw was all too much for my brain to handle) but somehow we ended up next to each other.

Well, this was going to be interesting.

'These guys are all coming to the Hotel Royale

Christmas Ball,' Skylar announced. 'I'll be flying back from LA especially.'

'It's one of the highlights of the year,' Ethan claimed. 'I love it.'

'You've only been once before.' Carly laughed.

'Yeah, and it was great. I'm sure it will be great this year too,' he said defensively.

'Did you all know that Flick actually lives here in the hotel?' Skylar informed the table excitedly. 'This is her *home.*'

'You live at Hotel Royale?' Ethan's eyes widened as he pulled in his chair. 'You must know everything there is to know about this place then.'

'Not really,' I said shyly, fiddling with the silver napkin ring.

'She has invaluable knowledge about the forks,' Jacob teased.

Skylar rolled her eyes. 'Ignore Jacob, Flick, he's pretending not to care but he's still smarting from losing out on a big modelling campaign today.'

'I couldn't care less,' he replied breezily, clearly lying. I know because he made the same trying-not-to-look-bothered face that Ella made whenever someone else got what she wanted, like the time Zoe got partnered with Aidan in a science project. I had to listen to her go on about how much she 'didn't care' for THREE DAYS and nod along while she made constant snide remarks about Zoe, until Aidan finally asked Ella on a date to the cinema and the whole world rejoiced in the change of her conversation.

'Ask him who he lost the campaign to, Flick.' Skylar laughed across the table to me as Carly sniggered.

'Who did you lose it to?' I asked.

Jacob sighed. 'Dolly.'

'And who is Dolly?' Skylar pushed, leaning forward on to the table and cupping her chin in her hands faux-innocently.

Jacob mumbled something.

'Sorry, what was that? I don't think Flick heard you,' Carly said, winking at Skylar.

Jacob clenched his jaw and said, through gritted teeth, 'A hamster.'

The table exploded into laughter.

'The brand decided to go in a different direction,' Jacob explained grumpily.

'The brand is clearly deluded.' Ethan chuckled, holding up his crystal glass of water. 'Anything with you as the face of it would sell in a second.'

'Hear hear! Or whatever it is you Brits say,' Skylar said as Jacob smiled, lifted his glass and clinked it with Ethan's.

Timothy came over to explain the menu and, after recommending the chef's specials, he left to give us time to decide. Skylar and Carly began to discuss Dolly's appeal with Jacob, and Ethan turned his attention to me.

'What was it like growing up here?' he asked.

'It was . . . uh . . . it was great,' I answered, wishing I had something more interesting to say.

'I bet this place has a cool history.'

'Yes. It does.'

'Fill me in.'

'Sorry?'

'On the history,' he explained enthusiastically. 'I love that kind of thing, and I've always been so intrigued about Hotel Royale. There's just something so . . . grand about this place. How did it all begin?'

I gulped.

Hotel Royale does have a really interesting history. I know that because I've heard people say it over and over again. When Mum talks about it, I do try really hard to be interested, but she can go on, and it's usually at really inconvenient times, like when I'm following a YouTube tutorial on curling my hair and trying not to burn my scalp. Stuff like that takes a lot of concentration. Mum never understands, though, and gets all naggy with me. I don't know why she thinks it's important for me to fill my brain with all those boring historical facts when I'm not the one in charge. Now, though, it would have been quite handy to impress Ethan with some hotel secrets. I was going to have to wing it. 'It was founded by my great-great-grandfather in the early 1900s,' I stated, which was a true story . . . I just didn't know what happened after that.

He nodded thoughtfully and I waited apprehensively for his question.

'Who runs it now?'

YES. I knew the answer to that one.

'My mum.'

'Wow,' he said, sounding genuinely impressed, for some reason. 'So it stayed in the family? Which means, you'll be taking the reins in the future, I'm guessing?'

I stared at him. 'Huh?'

'Unless you have any siblings?'

'No, just me.'

'So you'll be running this place one day.' He whistled, his glance sweeping across the dining room before coming round back to me. 'Not bad.'

'I haven't really thought about it,' I admitted with a shrug, fiddling with the menu.

'Seriously?' He looked stunned. 'Man, if it was me, that would be on my mind all the time.'

He picked up the menu and studied it.

'Every time I eat in this place, I can never decide what to pick. It all looks so good,' Ethan informed the table. I pretended to consider everything on the menu myself, even though most of it sounded gross. Duck liver? BLEUGH. Smoked eel? Ew! What was Chef thinking? I was going to have to have a word with him.

'You must know the menu off by heart,' Carly commented, smiling at me. 'Does it change a lot?'

'Not sure.'

They all looked surprised.

'You don't know about the menu in your own restaurant?' Ethan asked. 'But –'

Thankfully, Timothy arrived at that very moment to take our orders and I was let off the hook for a few minutes as he scribbled down our choices. As soon as he was done, I jumped in quickly to change the subject.

'Carly, did you do all the drumming on Skylar's album or just her tour?'

Carly happily launched into her answer and as everyone listened politely, I breathed a sigh of relief. I was getting a headache from all their questions.

'Flick, are you coming to Sky's London party?'

Skylar gasped at Ethan's question. 'That is such a good idea, Ethan! Yes, Flick, you've got to come. It's in a few weeks in, like, the *coolest* club in the city. Will you come?'

'Wow! I'd love to. Are you sure?'

'Yes, I'm sure.' Skylar laughed. 'You are my hostess after all, it would be rude not to invite you.'

'I can't believe you live here,' Carly said, shaking her head.

Oh no. Not this again.

'I know, right?' Skylar nodded. 'Imagine growing up in this place.'

'It's really not that big a deal,' I said quickly, taking a sip of water as my face grew hot again.

'Don't play it down.' Ethan smiled encouragingly. 'Tell us about it. Do you live in one of the suites?'

'Do you have your own butler?' Carly asked, leaning forward, fascinated.

'Do you order vats of ice cream from room service, like in *Home Alone 2*?' Jacob chuckled.

'Have you always held your birthday parties here? They must have been amazing.' Sky smiled. 'You must have met some amazing people too.'

'Hey, you should go on Ethan's vlog,' Jacob suggested.

'What a brilliant idea!' Skylar clapped her hands together as the other two nodded. 'What do you think, Ethan?'

'I think it sounds cool. Flick?' he said, as everyone waited for my answer. 'What do you say? Want to be a guest star on my vlog?'

That was when I saw Audrey, stopping at the door to proudly survey the scene and make sure everything was in order. If she saw me, she would come thundering over to the table and probably tell me to go to my room. I had already embarrassed myself enough this evening in front of the coolest people on the planet. If Audrey spotted me, my life would literally be over. There was only one thing to do. Without any explanation, I threw myself dramatically on to the ground and crawled under the table.

'Well . . .' I heard Ethan laugh, as the table fell into stunned silence. 'I think that might be a no.'

EIGHT

'That makes TOTAL sense. Everyone just thought you were really weird.'

I lifted the slices of cucumber from my eyes so I could look at Skylar.

'Did Ethan say that?'

'That you were weird? Yeah.'

I slumped into the reclining chair and closed my eyes, putting the cucumber slices back on my eyelids. It had been a few days since the disastrous dinner, and this was the first chance I'd had to explain myself.

I'd had to wait for ages for Audrey to leave, by which point the food had arrived and no one had been sure what to do. Skylar had peered under the tablecloth to find out what was going on but unfortunately, so had everyone else, and I couldn't tell them all (I mean, I was mainly thinking of Ethan 'the Jaw' Duke) the reason I was under there.

And I know I looked pretty stupid anyway, hiding underneath the table, but it was better than all of Skylar

Chase's glamorous friends thinking I was a big baby, being caught by Audrey and sent to my room.

When I saw Audrey's shoes leaving the restaurant, I decided that it was too risky to hang around there. She was bound to come back. It had been a stupid idea to agree to go to dinner with Skylar. If Audrey had seen me and told Mum, then the punishment would have been stretched out even longer. I was on strike two. As soon as I saw those polished Christian Louboutins clacking in the opposite direction, I crawled out from under the table, told everyone I had to go because of 'a thing' and then ran full-pelt towards the door that led to the piano room, before bursting through it and interrupting a cast of singers in the middle of a private performance.

'So, what did you do?'

'I picked up a fan from the props table and pretended to be part of the performance.'

'You did not!' Skylar screeched with laughter.

'I did. Why is it that whenever I go through that door, someone is in there?'

'I can't believe you hid under the table. You should have just explained the situation and excused yourself.'

'And look like a complete and utter loser? I bet none of your friends ever get grounded.'

'None of us ever attacked a prince.'

'I didn't attack him, I just hid in his wardrobe. There's a big difference.'

Skylar giggled before letting out a happy sigh. 'Isn't this the dream right now?'

I had to agree that it wasn't a bad night in. Skylar had put in a request with Audrey that I join her for a pampering evening, after she'd spent almost all week running around fashion shows in high heels in between her gigs. Apparently, London Fashion Week was no joke.

Skylar's PA had pretty much set up our own private spa in her room, complete with beauticians ready to give us manicures, pedicures, face masks and head massages. I'd been given a dressing gown and some kind of disgusting healthy green smoothie as soon as I'd walked through the door. I'd ditched the smoothie, but gladly hopped up on to the big reclining leather chair in my fluffy white gown.

I'm not sure if either the beauticians or Skylar had been expecting me to bring Fritz, but he was being particularly needy that afternoon, so I didn't have the heart to leave him alone in his basket. I made sure he came prepared for a pampering session, popping him in his own personal dressing gown, which he'd been given by the owner of a Covent Garden spa. The gown even had his name in gold stitching along the back and was perfect for cold winter evenings.

Skylar and her team had gone crazy when I arrived with him under my arm and they all fussed him so much that it got to his head – he ran into Skylar's bedroom and attempted to jump up on her bed, no doubt thinking he had been upgraded and that this was now his room. Unfortunately, his little legs couldn't quite scale the bed and he was left scrambling on the side of the sheets until Skylar picked him up and let him settle down on her lap for a nap. But not before we got a brilliant Instagram snap of him with his front paws in the foot massager.

'Do you do this kind of thing often?' I asked, picking a maroon nail polish from the selection Danielle, the beautician, was holding.

'Sadly not,' Skylar replied, stroking Fritz's head absent-mindedly. 'I don't have the time. But, trust me, it's essential during Fashion Week. No end of cameras, no end of new shoes. My feet are so blistered, they're falling off.'

'I'm so jealous.'

'Of the blisters?'

'Yes, I'm jealous of the blisters,' I said sarcastically, as she sipped her smoothie. 'No, of you going to Fashion Week. It must be amazing to see it all.'

'You've never been? I'm surprised.'

'Why?' I asked, watching my nails being filed down to perfect curves.

'Because you're Flick Royale,' she said, as though I was being stupid. 'I'm sure designers would love to have you watching their shows. You should just go.'

'Have you *met* my mum?' I sighed. 'She's so strict. One time, an actress staying here invited me and Fritz to a premiere of her latest film and Mum wouldn't let us go.'

'Why not?'

'It was the same night as Mum's birthday party.'

'Ah, well, that seems kind of fair.' Skylar laughed.

'Yeah, except she held this super boring dinner party with all these old people and I was stuck in between two men talking about the state of the economy.' I rolled my eyes at the horrific memory. 'That's why sometime soon I want to get a vlog going. At the moment, I never get to do anything cool.'

Sky looked at me curiously. 'What about tomorrow night?'

'What about it?' I said, lying back so that Danielle could start sponging my face mask off.

'I'll be at the fashion shows. Come with me. I'm sure they wouldn't mind adding you to their list.'

'Stop tempting me with such an amazing invite!' I moaned, though my heart soared at the thought. 'I can't leave the hotel.'

'You've never snuck out before?'

I let Danielle finish washing my face before I turned to Skylar. 'You're a terrible influence.'

'You bring it out in me.' She smiled mischievously. 'It's like having a little sister to lead astray.'

'I can't.'

'All right then.' She sighed. 'It's a shame that it's happening this week and not next week when you're free. Never mind, you can go next year.'

I groaned. Next year was so far away! And how often does the world's biggest pop star invite you to go with her to Fashion Week? NEVER. It was all so unfair, but there was no chance I would get away with it – there would be photos all over the Internet as soon as I stepped anywhere with Skylar. But this was a chance of a lifetime. It was surely worth it. What was the worst Mum could do?

'OK.'

Skylar looked at me blankly. 'OK, what?'

'OK, I'll come to Fashion Week with you tomorrow.'

A smile spread across her face. 'Really?'

'Yes. But it will have to be after I'm back from school, so just an evening show. And I'll have to make Mum think I'm upstairs doing my homework so she doesn't check on me.'

'Yes! Tomorrow night is Lewis Blume's show, and I have him on speed dial so I'll call and get you on the guest list. This is so exciting!' she cried, wriggling her pedicured toes and disturbing grumpy Fritz. He was not one to pander to celebrities. 'Although, how are you going to sneak out the hotel without being seen?'

I nestled snugly back into my chair and admired my shiny new nails.

'Leave that to me.'

Since meeting Skylar, school seemed duller than ever.

I kept getting told off in lessons for not paying attention. Most of the time I was daydreaming about appearing on Ethan's vlog and how jealous Ella and Grace would be when they found out. I had eventually told the girls that Skylar and I had spoken once or twice, which made me even more popular at school than I already was. I was constantly surrounded by people on the way to lessons and at break times. I happily told them that Skylar was very nice but I hadn't given anyone any more details yet, despite Grace questioning me every second of the day. I wasn't sure why, maybe because I was secretly terrified that it was all some kind of humiliating joke and Skylar was going to turn around and be like, 'You thought *we* were friends? Ew!'

It could happen.

All I told them was that I'd bumped into her in reception a few times and she seemed nice, which was enough for Grace and some of the other girls to scamper after me at every chance they got and ask whether or not I'd be seeing Skylar again, how long she was staying for, if she was going to the Christmas Ball, whether or not I'd be allowed to go to one of her gigs and take some friends with me and if so, who I would be taking.

'Do you think she'd mind if you asked her for some autographs?' Grace asked eagerly at the end of maths, as I gathered my books off the desk.

'She's really busy with Fashion Week. She doesn't have the time.'

'Oh, right.' Grace nodded, looking disappointed. 'Maybe after Fashion Week then.'

'Maybe. She's got a jam-packed schedule. Anyway, why don't you get Ella and we can go to lunch?'

'OK!' she said, before rushing off to stand outside Ella's classroom and wait for her.

I got to my locker, relieved to have some peace, and saw Oliver standing next to it.

'Hey.' He smiled as I approached. 'I thought my sister might be with you. I picked up one of her books by accident this morning, and she must have taken mine.'

He held up a plain black notepad and then opened it to show me a page covered in cutouts of Ethan Duke's face with red hearts scribbled around them.

'This page was a bit of a giveaway.'

'Right.' I laughed. 'You want me to give it to her?'

'I'm surprised she's left your side for a second. You're all she talks about these days. Well –' he hesitated, passing me the notepad – 'you, Ethan Duke and Skylar Chase.'

I saw him glance over my shoulder and turned to see Ella swanning towards us, with Grace one step behind.

'Hey, Oliver,' Ella said, fluttering her thick, mascara-covered eyelashes.

'Hey. Excited about tonight?'

She nodded. 'Can't wait.'

'What's tonight?' I asked without thinking.

'Ella's party,' Grace reminded me.

'Oh, right. I forgot it was tonight.'

'I wish you could come,' Grace said, looking at me sympathetically. 'Any chance you could sneak out?'

'That's a good idea . . . even if it did come from my sister,' Oliver added with a cheeky smile at Grace, who scowled back at him.

'I can't,' I replied quickly. 'Sorry.'

'Oh well.' Ella smiled sweetly up at Oliver. 'So, what time do you think you'll be getting there?'

I've come up with a plan

What are you talking about?
Aren't you meant to be at Ella's?

I'm being fashionably late. Ella told
me that was the thing to do

Grace, she probably won't be too
happy about you doing that for her party

Do you want to hear my plan?

What plan?

I cause a distraction at the hotel
and you creep out and then I cause
another distraction later for you to
sneak back in after the party. I know, right?
GENIUS

I can't. Thanks though

You haven't heard what the distraction is yet

Fine. What's the distraction?

My dad has a full Storm Trooper costume in his wardrobe, complete with a toy blaster. I can run through reception wearing it, waving the blaster gun around and everyone will be too busy worrying about chasing me to notice you creeping out. Then I come back in the costume a few hours later and yell "YOU THOUGHT YOU WERE RID OF ME, HUH?", they start chasing me again and that's when you sneak back in

WHAT? As in the bad guys from those Star Wars films?! Why does your dad have a STORM TROOPER costume?

He wore it to a themed birthday party, years ago. He has worn it every Christmas Day since. It's a family tradition

That is the weirdest thing I ever heard

So, whaddya say? Want me to go get the blaster?

112

NO GRACE I DON'T WANT YOU
TO GO GET THE BLASTER. Thanks, though.
It's a very nice and slightly disturbing offer

Party would be way more fun if you were there.
Let me know if you change your mind!

NINE

'*Lord of the Flies*,' Mum read aloud, picking up the book from my desk and stroking the front cover. 'I didn't know you were studying this.'

'Yep, got LOADS to do.' I'd already put on my tortoiseshell glasses, to help with the studious vibe.

She nodded, scanning her eyes over the notes and books scattered around my laptop.

'You look busy.'

'They're really piling on the homework this year,' I explained, pointing at my 'To Do' list, which I'd quickly scribbled earlier. 'I don't know how I'm going to finish this essay – it's due tomorrow. I'll be stuck here working on it all night.'

'Really? I love *Lord of the Flies*, maybe I can help. What's the essay question?'

'You've read *Lord of the Flies*? Isn't it a bit young for you?'

She perched on the edge of the desk. 'This was published in the 1950s, Flick. I read it as a teenager.'

'Oh, right. Well, the essay question is really boring and complicated, you probably don't want to bother with it,' I mumbled quickly, glancing at the time. I didn't have long before Skylar would be ready to pick me up.

'Try me.' Mum shrugged.

'What are the important symbols in *Lord of the Flies*?' I read out. 'See? Really tricky.'

'That's a great question. Let's see, you have –'

'OK, thanks, Mum, I know you're super busy and I wouldn't want to keep you.'

She looked slightly taken aback at the interruption but then rolled her eyes and stood up from the desk.

'All right, all right, I can take a hint. I've got to get to the other side of London for a book launch anyway. I won't be back late.'

She planted a kiss on my head and ruffled my hair. I smoothed it back into place as she went to my bedroom door.

'Flick,' she said, turning back, 'I know about tonight.'

'What?' I squeaked.

HOW COULD SHE KNOW? There was no way Skylar would have told her! *Do all mums have some sort of secret antennae that can sense when you're about to break their stupid rules?* I thought to myself. How was I going to get out of this one? Distract her with something worse! THINK, BRAIN, THINK!

'BLASTER!'

'What?'

NOT YOUR BEST WORK, BRAIN!

'The weapons the bad guys have in *Star Wars*. Blasters. They're awful. Don't you think?'

'Um. OK?' She looked more confused than ever.

ABORT MISSION!

'I was talking about Ella's party?' she said, looking at me strangely. 'It's tonight, right?'

'Oh. That.'

PHEW!

'I am sorry, you know. That you're missing out.'

'It's fine, don't worry about it.'

'Really, I mean it,' she said seriously. 'I appreciate that all your friends will be going but I hope you understand why I can't let you go.'

'Yeah, totally. I understand. Have fun tonight.' I nodded, wishing she would just leave.

'You're being really grown up about this, Flick. I'm proud of you.' Mum smiled before closing the door.

Wow. Could she have taken any longer to LEAVE? Old people really like to loiter.

As soon as I heard the *ding* of the lift doors opening in the corridor, I rushed over to my wardrobe, clumsily changing out of my pyjamas and pulling on one of my favourite mini dresses and a jacket to match. I put on some eyeliner and mascara as carefully as I could in a hurry, and then hunted down my black boots.

Fritz, who had been curled up in his basket, lifted his head and ears in interest as I trampled around my room – before stepping out and stretching, wagging his tail ready for a trip.

'Not today, Fritz,' I said, successfully locating one boot under my bed. 'You're going to have to stay here.'

His ears dropped and he sat forlornly.

'Don't be like that,' I grumbled, kneeling down to rummage through the bottom of my wardrobe for my other boot. 'I asked and Skylar said that dogs are not welcome at this show. Argh, where is my other boot?'

I sat back on my feet and scanned the room. I stopped when I got to Fritz's basket.

'Fritz,' I said in a warning tone, 'is that my boot in your basket?'

He blinked at me innocently. I reached forward to snatch my boot but as I grabbed it, Fritz lunged at the same time and gripped the boot in his jaws.

'Fritz, this is not the time to be difficult!'

I stood up and lifted my boot with me so that he would let go, but his grip was strong and he refused to drop it, instead coming with the boot and dangling in the air. I quickly dropped it so he wouldn't hurt himself and he triumphantly trotted back to his basket, plopping the boot in the centre and sitting on top of it.

My phone buzzed on the desk with a message from Skylar.

Hey, I'm waiting in the car. You on your way? Don't want to be late for the show. Sky x

'Fine,' I huffed, marching into the kitchen and picking up Fritz's dog bowl and bag of food. He plodded up curiously behind me. 'You win. If I give you another supper, will you let me leave?'

He tilted his head in agreement.

'There.'

I placed his bowl on the floor and he dived into it head first. I took the opportunity to rush back to my room, pull on my boot and shove my phone, keys and sunglasses into my pocket.

'I won't be long,' I called to him as I closed the door. He didn't look up once from his bowl.

118

According to the guests, there is one way to enter and exit Hotel Royale – through the large gold-plated revolving front door where a load of men and women wearing silly uniforms and top hats stand, greeting you and waving you off. According to the staff, there are three ways: the front door, a door that leads out from the kitchens into a back road for deliveries, and a door from the laundry rooms into a side road.

There also happens to be a fourth door. A *secret* door.

It was Cal's and my greatest discovery when we had been playing one of our favourite games a few years ago: 'steal-Chef's-hat-and-hide-it-where-he'll-never-find-it'. We had been racing away from Chef, laughing our heads off as he thundered after us still holding a whisk in his hand, confident in the knowledge that he'd never catch us. Cal and I could be speedy when we wanted to be. Our usual route was through the kitchens, out on to the back road and then on to the main road where we'd give it to a very pleased tourist who happened to be passing by. But one day, our route was blocked by delivery men with ginormous boxes of food.

Chef had laughed victoriously, folding his arms and going, 'No way out this time, suckers.'

Cal was all ready to hand back the hat and admit defeat but I wasn't going to let that happen, so I yelled at him to follow me and then darted round the kitchen, cutting Chef off from a straight path to us, and pelted into the maze of corridors underneath the hotel. We just kept running, dodging the staff rushing around on their duties, until we reached a dead end next to a random storeroom full of boxes and old broken furniture. Never even knowing it existed, we coughed our way to the back of the room through the dust.

'What now, genius?' Cal had laughed as we stood catching our breath against the back wall. 'Wait,' he said peering past me, 'what's that?'

He pointed at a thin slit of light in the corner of the room, which appeared to be coming through the wall. We moved closer and his eyes widened with excitement.

'It's a door! A secret one.' He moved his hands around the wall. 'It completely blends in.'

'Well, push it, dumdum.'

'I'm not pushing it. We don't know where it leads,' he replied nervously.

'You are such a chicken,' I huffed, elbowing him aside.

I pushed on the wall with all my strength and the door creaked open, letting sunlight pour in. It led to a tiny porch-like walled area with what looked like a wooden garden door on the other side. Cal went through and lifted the latch of the second door, poking his head out and then beaming at me. 'It's the back road.' He laughed. 'This leads to the back road!'

It was our proudest moment, and we made the most of our new secret. We spent ages tidying up the back of the storeroom so it wasn't so dirty – Cal's terrified of spiders so guess who had to dust the gross cobwebs up? – and then we even weeded the paving of the courtyard (which took us all of five minutes considering how small it was). Cal had done some nerdy research, of course, into the architecture of the hotel, and discovered that the exit had been used as an emergency escape by staff during the war, but it had since been forgotten. We never told anyone about it and used it all the time to sneak out or play tricks. I hadn't been there in years.

Until now.

I rushed through the hotel on full alert, careful not to let Audrey or Matthew see me. The hardest part was getting through the staff corridors unseen, but I got lucky with my timing: the chefs were all dashing about the kitchen sorting dinner and housekeeping must have been turning down beds for the evening. I managed to race to the storeroom without being noticed. I did a quick glance down the deserted corridor and slid through the door. Everything was exactly how it had been, except it was clean. Really clean. There were still stacks of wooden chairs and broken shelves dotted about the place, but it wasn't dusty, which was weird. Maybe Matthew or someone had started using it again for storage and had cleaned the place up. It was brighter in there than I remembered, with light pouring in through a window at the back. But there was still a makeshift pathway weaving around the junk, which was handy. As I got to the end of it, I accidentally knocked my arm on a chair, nudging it noisily across the floor.

A voice came from the back. 'Who's there?'

I screamed and darted backwards, knocking my head on a wardrobe.

'Careful! Are you OK?'

Cal appeared looking concerned.

'What are you doing here?' I hissed, rubbing the bump forming on my head.

'I could ask you the same thing,' he replied, crossing his arms. I looked past him at where he'd been and saw his laptop perched on a big, cushioned armchair.

'What the . . . What is this?'

I took in all the cushions on the armchair and the stacks of books lying around it. There were way too many books lying around for him to have brought them along in his backpack in one trip. He was not here on a one-off.

'Wait a second, do you work down here?'

He sighed and ran a hand through his hair. 'Yeah. I do.'

I looked up at him in confusion. 'Since when?'

'Most of last year, and when I was writing during the summer.'

'Why?'

'It's loud at home,' he explained. 'Mum is always on the phone to her clients and our next-door neighbour is learning the drums. I can't think there.'

'So you just set up . . . *here*?'

He shrugged. 'I never get disturbed.'

'You've made it kind of cosy, I have to say.'

'Thanks.' He smiled.

My phone started buzzing in my pocket.

'Gotta go.'

'Aren't you grounded?' he asked, suddenly looking me up and down. 'You look dressed up.'

'Good luck with the rest of your work!' I said, kicking aside some of his books to get to the door. 'I'll need to get back in this way later, so if you could make sure the passageway is clear that would be great.'

'Wait a second, you're sneaking out?'

'Good detecting, Sherlock. See ya.'

'Flick, wait.' He reached forwards and grabbed my arm. 'You can't sneak out! It's a really stupid idea. Ella's party is not worth the hassle.'

'I'm not going to Ella's party,' I said, shaking off his hand.

'Well, then, where are you going?'

I pushed open the secret door to the courtyard, noting it was nowhere near as stiff as it used to be. Cal must have greased the hinges. 'Nowhere, just don't tell anyone.'

'Flick, would you just listen to me for one sec–'

'Wait, what is this?'

I cut him off as I took in what the door had opened out to. What had once been a very small concrete courtyard, was now a mini garden. There was climbing ivy across the walls, and flower boxes lining the paving.

'I did some gardening last year,' Cal answered, coming to stand next to me and lean on the door frame. My phone vibrated again with another missed call from Skylar, and a message flashed up when I checked the screen.

WHERE ARE YOU? Did you make it?
We're going to be late if you
don't get your butt here soon!

I was about to put it back in my pocket when another message came through.

P.S. Hope your mom didn't catch you???

124

'Hold on.' Cal peered over my shoulder. '"Mom"?'

'Didn't anyone ever tell you it was rude to read other people's messages?' I huffed, taking a step outside.

'The only American you know is Skylar Chase.' Cal stepped out after me. 'Flick, this is a really bad idea. You'll easily get caught if you're going anywhere with her. She's hardly subtle. It will be in the *Daily Post* the minute you walk outside.'

'So?'

'So, your mum will kill you. Whatever stupid thing you're doing, just leave it and go out next week.'

'You are such a goody-goody.'

'Fine,' he said, his concerned expression disappearing as he stomped back inside. 'Go ahead and be an idiot. I won't try to stop you.'

'Like you could,' I sneered.

I opened the latch and peeked outside. A black car with tinted windows was waiting on the side of the road. The car horn beeped. I waved, and then turned back to Cal.

'Leave the door propped open, will you? One of those heavy books will do,' I said, before darting out without waiting for him to reply and jumping into the back of the car.

Skylar was sitting on the back seat wearing

sunglasses and bright red lipstick. She leaned across to give me a hug.

'You made it! Was it OK? Any problems?'

'None whatsoever,' I said smugly, whipping my sunglasses out my pocket and putting them on. 'Let's go.'

TEN

Cameras began flashing the moment our car drew up outside the venue. Skylar took a deep breath.

'Keep your sunglasses on until we're inside,' she advised. 'They do formal photographs once you're through and we can take them off then. But for the walk to the door, trust me, you'll want to be able to see where you're going, without flashes in your face.'

I nodded and the driver opened the car door, presenting his hand to Skylar as she stepped out with her winning smile. I shuffled across the seat and followed suit, allowing the driver to help me out, attempting to be as elegant as possible. Skylar linked her arm through mine and, waving at the photographers, she led me towards the building. She was right about the blinding flashes but she hadn't warned me about the noise. All the reporters were yelling over each other, desperate to catch our attention and lure us over for an interview: 'Skylar, over here!'; 'Skylar, who's your friend?'; 'Skylar, is it true that you're appearing on a British reality TV show? Which one?';

'Ladies, look this way!'; 'Skylar, how do you feel about your ex moving on?'; 'Skylar, are you buying a London house?'; 'Girls, whose after-party will you be attending?'; 'Who are you wearing? Are you wearing Lewis Blume?'; 'Skylar, is Lewis Blume your favourite designer?'

The reporters continued to take pictures and fire off questions until we were safely inside.

'Whoa,' I gushed, once the doors closed behind us. 'What a rush! I couldn't see a thing through all those flashes, though.'

'I know, right? Sunglasses vital. Ah, there he is!'

Skylar took off her Wayfarers and held her arms out as Ethan Duke came strolling towards us. He was wearing a black leather jacket over a white T-shirt and the skinniest black jeans I'd ever seen.

'You've arrived! And look who you've brought. No tables for you to hide under this time, Flick.' He smiled, leaning in to give me a kiss on both cheeks. He was so sophisticated, you'd think he was way older than sixteen. Plus his aftershave smelled so good, it made my brain go fuzzy.

'Yeah, sorry about that. I don't normally do that kind of thing.'

'Duck under a table and then run away as the starters arrive?'

'Yep. That.'

'Understandable when you're trying not to get caught breaking house arrest.' He winked at Skylar.

I rounded on her.

'You told him?' I hissed, the heat rising to my cheeks.

'It's better than everyone thinking you dodge questions by leaping under tables!'

Ethan watched us, bemused.

A woman wearing a lanyard and holding an iPad interrupted to usher us over to a screen covered in Lewis Blume's name, so that we could pose for the photographers. Having already been photographed, Ethan excused himself and joined a circle of incredibly beautiful people nearby. I assumed the photographers would want Skylar on her own, so I took a step back while she put a hand on her hip and looked at them over her shoulder. She looked so slick and professional.

'And Miss Royale, if you could step forwards now?' the woman with the iPad instructed.

'Me?'

'Yes, of course,' she said, smiling. 'There'll be more when you're seated, too, but if we could just get some full-length shots of you and Miss Chase, that would be great.'

'Come on, Flick,' Skylar said, holding out her hand.

I thought about keeping my cover for the tiniest

second . . . but then a camera flashed my worries away. This. Was. Awesome. I took Skylar's hand and eagerly stepped in line next to her, mirroring her pose with a hand on my hip.

'You're a natural.' Skylar laughed as the photographers thanked us and we moved aside to let them snap the next arrivals.

'It's so much fun!' I said, looking around eagerly. 'I recognise everyone in here. Look, Ethan is talking to Marianne Montaine.'

'Let's go take our seats,' Skylar said chirpily, taking a photo of the crowd and posting it online.

I followed her to the benches lining the runway and tried to act as though I did this sort of thing all the time, which was VERY difficult, especially when I spotted a reality TV star holding hands with someone who was NOT her boyfriend.

'OMG!' I gasped, giving Skylar's sleeve a sharp tug and nodding my head in their direction. 'In the last episode, she was dating that Aaron guy who owned the French Bulldog!'

'Who? What are you talking about?' Skylar followed my gaze but still looked confused.

'The best show on TV! You might not get in America but basically *she* was hanging out with this guy, Matt, who everyone could see was all wrong for her because the only thing he talked about was his strawberry protein shakes, and then Aaron came along who was way more down to earth and . . . uh . . .' I hesitated as Skylar stared at me blankly.

So much for playing it cool.

'Never mind,' I said hurriedly, flicking my hair over my shoulder and changing the subject. 'Fashion shows are just sooo tiring.'

The lady with the iPad came over to lead us to our seats, gesturing to where our name labels were propped up next to each other on the bench.

'Enjoy the show,' she said brightly, hurrying off to escort everyone else to their seats.

'The only problem with front row,' Skylar began, sitting down and crossing her legs, 'is that you're constantly on show.'

'You say that like it's a bad thing,' I replied, taking my place next to her and buzzing with excitement as heads turned to look at us.

'You can't let your guard down for a second. Trust me.' She gave me a knowing look. 'Someone once got a photo of me yawning and then I got a phone call from the designer the next day, asking me why I didn't like her collection. I loved it! I was just jet-lagged but the reporters made it seem like I was bored.'

'So, just perfect smiles the whole time.' I grinned as a group of people sitting opposite stared across at us, whispered to each other and then began lifting up their phones to take photos. 'That won't be a problem today.'

'Picture?' a photographer said, crouching down in front of us and holding up his camera. 'If you could just lean towards each other – that's perfect. Thank you.' He clicked away as I tilted my head towards Skylar and smiled. 'Ah, excellent, and now the three of you?'

'Three of us?'

'Absolutely,' came a familiar voice. Ethan sat down next to me and leaned in for the shot.

He smelled so good. And his knee was touching my knee. And his arm was warm against my arm. And he smelled so good. Did I already say that?

'That'll be a keeper,' Ethan stated confidently as the photographer moved on. 'I might get that framed.'

I laughed nervously in reply before the lights on the audience lowered and upbeat music blared from the speakers. Models began filing on to the catwalk and everyone got out their phones, probably posting updates on social media every second. I quickly took mine from my pocket and began snapping away too, not wanting to miss a moment.

Suddenly Ethan squeezed my hand, taking me by surprise and instantly making my palms all sweaty and gross. ARGH, WHY DOES SWEAT EXIST?

I should start carrying a portable fan for whenever I bump into Ethan Duke, and just permanently aim it at my palms.

As he gripped my hand, he said, 'There he is,' excitedly, pointing at one of the models emerging for his moment on the catwalk. It wasn't until he was a bit closer that I realised it was Jacob – I almost didn't recognise him with his eyes covered in black make-up and his hair dyed peroxide blond. I looked back down dreamily at Ethan's fingers wrapped through mine and wondered whether it would be weird to take a photo of them. Just as I was trying to work out how I could take a picture of our hands without him noticing, Ethan let go to applaud his friend as he passed.

Clapping is a stupid tradition.

When the designer, Lewis Blume, came out from backstage at the end, Skylar jumped to her feet applauding and whooping, so I did the same. He bowed to the applause several times and then singled Skylar out and came over to grasp her hands in his and give her a kiss on the cheek. He disappeared backstage again and as the lights came up, everyone stood to leave, chatting about the collection and taking more photos.

'You ready to go backstage?' Skylar said, nodding at iPad lady who beckoned us to follow her.

'How do you know Lewis Blume so well, Skylar?' I asked, keeping up with her as she strode towards iPad lady, while typing rapidly into her phone.

'He's designed so many of my tour costumes and award-night dresses,' she answered without looking up. 'He practically moved in when he was in America, he designed so much of my wardrobe. He's the king of British fashion. And you can call me Sky, you know. Skylar's a bit formal.'

YES! WE ARE OFFICIALLY FRIENDS.

'Right, sure. Sky,' I said coolly, as though I hadn't really thought about it.

We were shown backstage, where Lewis Blume was ready to greet Sky with open arms, gushing about how divine she looked, desperate to know if she liked the new collection. She enthusiastically assured him it was the best collection he'd ever done and then, after Lewis had greeted Ethan warmly, he turned his attention to me.

'Have you met Flick Royale?' Sky began. 'I'm staying at her mother's beautiful hotel while I'm in the UK.'

Lewis launched into praise about the hotel and took my hand in his to kiss it, while I tried to get a word in to tell him how much I liked his show.

'You know,' he said, looking at me intensely. 'Your mother is a remarkable woman. Remarkable. There's nowhere like Hotel Royale. Nowhere in the whole world.'

'Thank you,' I answered, wondering whether he realised he hadn't let go of my hand.

'Any time you need a dress, you call me.'

'OK.' I beamed. 'I will.'

'Ah!' he cried, releasing my hand to clap his together and taking a step back to look me up and down. 'I would love to dress you. It is an honour to have you attend my show. Send your mother my love and tell her that I can't wait for the Hotel Royale Christmas Ball. It is the party of the season. And tell her that if she needs a dress, she knows where to come.'

I laughed. 'I'll pass on the message.'

He blew us all kisses and went to greet Victoria Beckham who had come through to congratulate him. My phone went and I grimaced when I saw that it was from Audrey.

Photos of you at Lewis Blume's show all over the Internet. Get back here asap. Your mum is on her way back from her launch. And that skirt is much too short.

> I'll ask housekeeping to lower your hem Love, Audrey xx

> Is Mum really cross?

> Yes. Love, Audrey xx

> Will head back home now

> Great. Love, Audrey xx

> Btw, you don't need to put 'Love Audrey' at the end of all of your messages. I know they're from you, I have your number saved

> Don't be cheeky. Love, Audrey xx

'There's an after-party if you're interested,' Sky told me before throwing her arms around Jacob who had made a beeline for us. I hugged him, mentioning that he was way better on the catwalk than a hamster could ever be, and then pulled Sky away to talk to her privately while Ethan stepped forwards to congratulate Jacob.

'I have to go.' I waved my phone screen under Sky's nose. 'I've been busted.'

Sky bit her lip. 'Is she angry?'

'Let's just say I don't think I'll be attending any after-parties any time soon.'

'And you'll be ducking under many more tablecloths?'

'Right.' I smiled, rolling my eyes. 'I'll call a taxi.'

Sky nodded and turned back to Ethan, who was now standing on his own watching Jacob pose for photos with another model from the show.

'Flick's got to go home,' Sky explained.

'I can drop you if you like,' Ethan offered quickly, his expression serious. 'I've got a driver. He'll be waiting right outside.'

'No, you don't need t–'

'It's not a problem, I'm leaving anyway.'

'You're not coming to the after-party?' Sky asked, looking confused.

'No,' Ethan said gravely. 'Have a good time, though. Come on, Flick, let's get going before your mum sends out a search party.'

Sky wished me luck and Ethan put his hand on the small of my back to guide me through the crowd. The paparazzi were still waiting outside and they leaped into action as we came out of the show, flashes going off everywhere. As it was darker now, I hadn't thought to put my sunglasses on – so I was immediately blinded by the flashing lights. Luckily Ethan was a pro at this kind of thing, and walked in front of me so I could look down and follow his shoes as he stepped confidently through the chaotic sea of photographers. His feet stopped suddenly and a car door swung open. Ethan held it as I clambered in and then slid in next to me, slamming the door behind him. 'Hotel Royale first, please,' he said to the man behind the wheel, who carefully pulled the car out into the road.

I watched the reporters lower their cameras, check the shots and then launch back into a frenzy as the door of the building opened again and someone else emerged.

'You must be used to that kind of thing.' I smiled, fiddling with the buckle of my seat belt.

'Not really.'

'Isn't that part of what you do, though? The whole being-on-camera thing?'

'Yeah,' he replied thoughtfully. 'It's different when you're not in control, though. With my vlogs, I'm in charge of what is being filmed and how it gets edited. I ask all the questions and decide on the angle. Being photographed like that, you never know what they're going to write about you under the pictures.'

'Better than not being written about,' I pointed out. 'Isn't there that saying? Any publicity . . .'

'Is good publicity,' he finished. He looked down at his hands with his forehead creased. 'I'm not so sure. You should see some of the stuff people leave in the comments on my channel. I always feel scared about what they'll say.'

'People say mean things?'

'Yeah, all the time.'

I stared at him. 'What mean thing can anyone possibly say about *you*?'

'Plenty, trust me.' He smiled weakly.

I hesitated. Ethan had been so cool and confident up until now, it was weird to see him like this. Like a normal teenager, worried about a piece of homework or something.

'Who cares what those mean people say?' I said firmly, attempting to be useful. 'Your fans definitely don't. If you need any evidence of that, then you should just come to my school sometime. No one there has anything bad to say, I can assure you.'

He laughed. 'Is that right?'

'Are you kidding? You'd be ambushed. You shouldn't worry about the bad comments. You've done so well being yourself, you should just keep doing that.'

Urgh, could I have been more cliché? That sounded like something Cal Weston would say. What a loser.

I opened my mouth to apologise for saying something so lame but the driver suddenly announced that we were home, and I felt my stomach drop.

'You OK?' Ethan asked. 'You've gone pale.'

'I don't want to go in.' I sighed. 'It's been such a fun evening, I don't want to be home.'

'And thus, Cinderella returned from the ball,' Ethan said dramatically, making me laugh. He flashed me a warm smile. 'You'll be all right.'

I nodded and was about to undo my seat belt when he put his hand gently on my arm.

'Speaking of which, you don't have a date to the Christmas Ball, do you?'

RUB IT IN WHY DON'T YOU. Brilliant. He clearly thinks I'm this totally undateable weird little loser, who hides under tables and says lame things like 'be yourself'. How embarrassing.

'Nope. I don't.'

'Want to go?'

'I have to go,' I replied, looking at him in confusion. 'It's my party. Well, my mum's.'

'I mean, together,' he said slowly, as though talking to a dim-witted monkey. 'Everyone seems to be going with a date this year and I don't have one – I was just wondering if you wanted to go together?'

'W-w-what?' I croaked, my mouth suddenly very dry.

'You're really going to make me explain it for a third time?' he asked, raising his eyebrows.

'No, no, course not,' I said quickly, shaking my head. 'That . . . er . . . that would be great.'

'Cool. Don't look so scared. We're friends, right?'

'Right. Yes. That's right. Friends. Great, friends. I mean, "great, we're friends", not "great friends" because you know, obviously, we haven't known each other that long so it would be impossible to be *great* friends, rather than just . . . friends.'

OH MY GOD STOP TALKING.

'Anyway,' I continued, 'what I mean is . . . yes. Friends.'

'Good. Would be pretty cool to go to the Hotel Royale Ball with a Royale.' He smiled, making my knees go weak. I moved to get out of the car but forgot to undo my seat belt. I was jerked backwards, prompting Ethan to burst out laughing.

Sure. I had to choose THAT MOMENT in front of a boy with THAT JAW who had just asked me on a DATE to completely forget the basic knowledge that a seat belt straps you into a seat. Thank goodness there were no reporters lurking around the hotel.

No one can ever know that happened.

I quickly unclipped the seat belt and clambered out on to the pavement.

'Hey,' he said, leaning over the back seat on to his elbow to peer up at me. 'It was really nice talking to you. There aren't many people I feel I can open up to. And I've never met anyone so adept with a seat belt before.'

'If you're not careful, I might be the one who starts writing mean comments on your vlogs.'

He grinned. 'See you around, Flick.'

I shut the door and the car drove off, leaving me standing outside the main door. I was about to be in big trouble but I couldn't stop smiling.

'Evening, Miss Royale,' the doorman said, as I walked up the steps. 'Good night?'

'The best,' I replied, before going through the revolving door where Mum was waiting for me.

ELEVEN

OMG OMG OMG OMG
OMG OMG OMG OMG
OMG OMG OMG OMG
OMG OMG OMG OMG
OMG OMG OMG OMG
OMG OMG OMG OMG
!!!!!!!!!!!!!!!!!!!!!!!!!!!

Hi Grace

WHY DIDN'T YOU TELL ME?

Tell you what?

SKYLAR CHASE AND ETHAN
DUKE!!!! WHAT IS
HAPPENINGGGGGGGGGG?

You probably need to lie down

143

OK. I AM LYING DOWN

Are you already home from Ella's party then? How was it?

I'M STILL AT THE PARTY

And you're lying down?

YES

Where?

THE FLOOR

At the party? You're lying on the floor in the middle of the party?

YES

That must look weird to everyone else there

THERE HAVE BEEN COMMENTS

The caps lock is kind of
hurting my eyes

I DON'T CARE. TELL ME.
BE QUICK. SOMEONE JUST SPILLED
A DRINK ON ME

I'll tell you everything at school.
If I'm ever allowed to leave my room

YOUR MUM CROSS AT YOU FOR
SNEAKING OUT?

Yeah. Big time

WHO CARES? YOUR BFF IS SKYLAR
CHASE. AND YOUR BOYF IS ETHAN
DUKE. SOMEONE JUST DROPPED A
SAUSAGE ROLL ON ME

Grace. Get up off the floor.
I promise to fill you in at school,
OK? I'll tell you everything.
Enjoy the party

∂ ♡ ✶

Mum and I sat in silence for a very long time. As soon as I'd walked into the hotel, she'd just pointed at the lift without saying anything and then stood inside with me, still not saying a word. We got to our floor and I sheepishly followed her into the flat where she simply pointed again, this time at the sofa. I sat down nervously.

And then it was just silent for ages.

Actually, that's a lie. It was like that for about four seconds until I heard Fritz's scrambling paws come pattering from my bedroom. He saw that we had returned and excitedly bounded over to climb up my leg.

'Not now, Fritz.'

Mum's low, stern voice echoed round the room. Fritz immediately stopped jumping and ran back to my room, his tail in between his legs.

And *then* it was silent for ages.

I'd never quite realised before just how excruciating silence is, especially when it's not a boring silence, but a terrifying, bad, bad silence. I watched her as she put her head in her hands, then she pinched her nose and concentrated for a bit. I thought she might be waiting for me to make the first move.

'I can expla—'

I thought wrong. Mum sharply held up her hand. I stopped talking. She inhaled deeply and opened her eyes to meet mine.

'What I can't understand, Flick,' she said slowly, 'is why you wouldn't talk to me about this.'

'About the fashion show?'

'Yes. About the fashion show.'

'Because,' I began, slumping back on to the cushions, 'you wouldn't have let me go.'

Her expression softened. 'Flick, do you know why I'm so upset?'

'Because I broke the rules.'

'You're wrong.'

I didn't say anything.

'I'm upset because nobody knew where you were. Audrey, Matthew and I, we all thought you were upstairs studying and you were in fact in a completely different part of London.'

'So?'

'So!' I saw a flash of anger cross her face. 'What if something had happened? Something in the hotel? Nobody would have known where you were! Can you imagine how worried we'd have all been?'

'Mum, I had my phone on me. It really is not that dramatic.' I picked up one of the cushions and clutched it to my chest.

'Flick,' she said, so quietly I could hardly hear her, 'you are being incredibly selfish.'

'I get what you're saying.' I sighed. 'But nothing bad happened and the whole world knew where I was, because it was all over the Internet. So it's not like I just disappeared.'

'Do. Not. Pull. A. Stunt. Like. This. Again.' She exhaled.

'I won't. And I'm sorry that I sneaked out when I was grounded. But it is Fashion Week and this was my only chance, and it wasn't just anyone who asked me to go with her, it was Skylar Chase. I didn't have much of a choice.'

'You should have told me. We could have compromised.'

'Whatever.'

'Flick,' she snapped, 'I would have listened to you. I am aware that it was quite the invitation. But you do not lie and sneak out. Next time you have a dilemma, you come to me and we talk it through, and come to a compromise.'

'Right.' I snorted. 'Like you would have let me go.'

'I would have considered it. I would have given you boundaries and rules, but I would have considered letting you go.'

'Even though I was grounded?'

'Yes.'

'Sure.' I put the cushion back in the corner and sat up. 'Can I go to my room now? I expect that's the order coming next. I'm tired anyway.'

She ran a hand through her hair and then stood up to gain the advantage of looking down at me as she delivered her final verdict. I knew the score.

'You've taken it too far this time,' she said, shaking her head.

'Really? Further than the Prince-Gustav thing?'

'I am in *no* mood for jokes, Flick. Don't try it.'

I crossed my arms stubbornly.

'From now, you are grounded for a month.'

No surprises there, then.

'And you are not allowed to attend the Christmas Ball.'

Wait. WAIT.

My jaw dropped. 'What?'

'You're not going to the Christmas Ball.'

'Mum, you can't –'

'I don't think you understand, Flick,' she barked.

It wasn't a shout, but it was definitely a raised voice, and that had never happened. I froze in my seat, my stomach tightening and my eyes welling with tears. She'd never spoken to me like this before.

'This wasn't just you mucking around, as usual,' she

continued through gritted teeth, 'this was you worrying me sick because you didn't know anyone you were with and anything could have happened.'

'I know Sky,' I whispered, a tear rolling down my cheek.

'For hardly *two weeks*!' she cried. 'You are my daughter, and for all I know, she could have left you stranded. Gone off without you. Left you to get home on your own, in the middle of nowhere. Anything.'

'She wouldn't do that.'

'How. Do. You. Know?'

I sniffed and looked down at my feet.

'Grounded for another month, no parties, no dinners in the restaurant with celebrity guests – yes, I know all about that, I'm not stupid – no weekends out with your friends, no going to Skylar Chase's concerts, certainly no vlogging and no Christmas Ball.'

'But I have a date!'

'No dates.'

'To the ball. Not just any date either but with –'

'You'll have to cancel. Now –' she folded her arms – 'I'm done. You can go to your room.'

Only I didn't go to my room. I was so upset by everything, I went to the lift and went down to Audrey's office, where she was sitting behind her desk shuffling through some papers. She stood up when she saw me in her doorway.

'Flick?'

I ran into her arms and burst into tears. She stroked my hair while I sobbed all over her dress.

'It's OK,' she repeated gently. 'Come on, sit down. Tell me what happened.'

She passed me a tissue as I sat in her big chair and then perched on the desk to listen to me. I filled her in on everything that Mum had said and burst into fresh tears when I got to the bit about the Christmas Ball, highlighting how bad it was because Ethan Duke had asked to go with me and I'd never fancied anyone before because all the boys at school were gross and this was a really big deal and now Mum was ruining my life.

'I see.' She nodded, listening to me patiently. 'But your mum has already told you what to do.'

'Yeah, stay in my room, shrivel up and die.'

'No, Flick,' she said, suppressing a smile. 'Make a compromise.'

I blew my nose. 'What do you mean?'

'Your mum is very reasonable. Right now she's only angry because she cares.'

'That old chestnut,' I said, rolling my eyes.

'Yes, that absolutely true old chestnut.' She passed me

another tissue as I threw my scrunched up one at her bin and missed. 'You know your mum better than anyone. You can't just throw a tantrum and demand that you're allowed to go to the Christmas Ball; that's not the way to go about things.'

'Huh,' I said thoughtfully, 'that's how I usually go about things.'

'I'm very well aware of that.' Audrey laughed. 'And how has that been working out for you recently?'

I considered her question. 'Not the best.'

'I thought as much. You've got to prove to her that you *deserve* to go to the ball.'

'How am I going to do that?' I whined. 'Buy her flowers and stuff?'

'No, show her that you're truly sorry, you've learned your lesson and that you can be responsible.'

'That sounds like hard work.'

Audrey smiled. 'Depends how you do it.'

'Any suggestions?'

'Oh, I have a suggestion, all right. A good one. One that, if you pull it off, will win your mum over, no doubt about it.'

'What is it?'

'You're not going to like it.'

'I'll do anything,' I pleaded. 'I have to go to the

152

Christmas Ball. It's Ethan Duke! This is a matter of life and death. What do I have to do to prove to Mum that I deserve to go?'

She took a deep breath and told me.

You have GOT to be kidding.

TWELVE

I was so preoccupied with what Audrey had said that I completely forgot to think about how people at school would react to the whole Skylar Chase thing.

The minute I walked through the gates, I was pounced on by EVERYONE. Students from every year group ran over and surrounded me, shouting questions and taking pictures. It took me about half an hour to get to the door of the main building, I was so in demand.

I should have been expecting the fuss; the picture of me, Sky and Ethan Duke sitting front row had spread across social media like wildfire. The *Daily Post* announced I was 'a new face on the social scene' and a fashion blogger referred to me as 'the hotel heiress with a *suite* sense of style'. I like what she did there.

When I left the hotel to get to school, all the photographers, who were usually waiting for Sky or someone, leaped into action and started taking photos of *me*, asking how long Skylar Chase and I had been friends for, and whether I would be joining her at any more events while she was in London. I didn't answer any of them but my jaw was aching from all the smiling by the time they left me alone. I would have to check those photos online later and hope that my school uniform didn't look too hideous.

I had spent most of the weekend trawling through websites, analysing every picture there was. I concluded that they were all acceptable but I should have spent more time on my eye make-up; it looked a bit smudged in the photos, but then, according to fashion bloggers, I was sporting the 'smoky-eye' look, as opposed to the 'did-my-mascara-badly-in-a-rush' look, so I think I got away with it.

Sky was performing at the O2 over the weekend, so I didn't see her, but she did leave a bouquet of flowers for me at reception, with a note saying how sorry she was that she'd got me into trouble. She even left a bouquet for Mum too, explaining that she'd encouraged me to go with her to the fashion show and she intended to apologise in person when she saw her. I watched Mum reading the note. She definitely looked impressed, and for a fleeting moment I thought that it might be enough to persuade her to forgive me. But no such luck.

It looked like I would have to go through with Audrey's suggestion after all.

'There you are!'

Grace was practically jumping up and down on the spot when I got to my locker, where she was waiting with Ella. I couldn't help but smile as Grace beamed up at me.

'So,' Ella said, moving aside to let me open my locker door, 'we have a LOT to talk about.'

'I know.'

'Olly – where do I even start?' Ella swooned. 'He's amazing.'

'Olly?'

I was confused. Didn't she mean Ethan?

'That's what he prefers to be called,' Ella explained, twisting a lock of her hair. 'We talked all night.'

'And they *snogged*,' Grace mumbled as it dawned on me that we were talking about her brother.

'Did you know he writes the band's songs as well as playing the guitar?' Ella continued. 'He is so talented. And it's only a hobby; he doesn't actually want to be a musician when he's older. He wants to go into politics or law.'

I attempted to look impressed but, HELLO, had she been under a rock this weekend? Hadn't she seen the pictures? Who cared about *Olly*?

'Cool,' I said, indulging her. After all, I guess I had stolen her thunder at her party so it was only fair that

I let her be the centre of attention for a bit.

'Anyway, Flick,' Grace began, clearly keen to move the conversation away from lovey-dovey rubbish about her sibling. 'You have to tell us everything! I can't believe you went to Lewis Blume's show. He's like the biggest designer ever!'

'I haven't heard of him,' Ella remarked, examining her cuticles.

I looked at her, baffled. Literally last week she'd been boring me about how much she loved his stuff and boasting that her mum was going to buy her one of his coats for her birthday.

'Is it true you're dating Ethan Duke?' Grace said, gripping my arm, distracting me from Ella's comment.

'Well, I –'

'Obviously not, Grace!' Ella interrupted. 'They only met that day.'

'We actually met before,' I corrected her. 'We had dinner in the hotel. Not just us two, with a group of Sky's friends. I was going to tell you.'

'You call her Sky!' Grace squealed. 'That is so cool! You're proper friends.'

'Anyway,' Ella said breezily, flicking her hair behind her shoulders, 'I've got to go. I told Olly I'd meet him before class.'

Grace watched her stalk off and then turned to me with a reassuring smile.

'Well, *I* think it's cool, anyway.'

'Thanks, Grace.'

'All weekend she's been going on about kissing with tongues.' Grace winced. 'I have to keep reminding her she's talking about my brother. It's SO gross.'

I suddenly spotted Cal come in and walk straight towards the library. I hurriedly pulled out the last of my books and slammed my locker door shut before everything came tumbling out.

'Sorry, Grace, I have to go,' I said quickly, watching Cal disappear through the library doors. 'Talk later, OK?'

'Can't wait!' Grace happily shouted after me as I raced to follow him, pushing through the squeaky doors at the end of the hallway and into the deathly silence of the library.

The library has always made me nervous. It really creeps me out because it's too big and quiet in there, plus the librarian, Mr Grindle, hates me because of that time he caught me doing an impression of his walk. It's not my fault he moves like an ostrich. Mr Grindle was reading as I came in and he did a double take at me when he looked up from his book.

'Felicity!' he said, bookmarking his page and

leaning forwards on his desk. 'Can I help you?'

I shook my head. 'Nope. Just perusing.'

'Perusing,' he repeated curiously, as though I'd presented him with a riddle.

'Yep. Having a look around.' You'd think a librarian would have a greater grasp of the English language.

'Would you like me to recommend you something?'

'No, I'm good. Thanks.'

'May I remind you that the library is a sanctuary of study and *peace*. Two things I'm not sure you've much experience of,' he said, all snootily.

This is why I hate the library. Because people like this hang out there.

'If you're planning on playing some kind of prank or causing trouble,' he continued, 'I suggest that you rethink it.'

'I'm not causing any trouble, just searching for a . . . book.'

'I see. Well then. Search away.'

'Thanks.'

I hurried down the centre pathway, glancing left and right down each empty row, aware that I remained under Mr Grindle's suspicious gaze. I came to a sudden halt when I spotted Cal at the end of the history section, reading with his headphones on. I sidled up next to him and coughed. When he didn't react, I pulled one of his headphones from his ear and pinged it back on to his head.

'Ow!'

Startled, he pulled his headphones down around his neck and glared at me.

'What are you doing?'

'I need your help.'

'Shh!' Mr Grindle suddenly appeared at the end of the row, pressing a finger to his lips. How did he get there so fast? His ostrich legs are more effective than I thought.

I mouthed 'sorry' and he strode back to his desk.

'What are you doing in here?' Cal whispered. 'You hate the library.'

'No, I don't,' I said defensively. 'I love the library.'

'Since when?'

'Since now. Who wouldn't love all these . . . dusty books?'

'What do you want, Flick? I'm busy.'

'Busy doing what?'

He tapped the page of the book open in his hands. 'Reading. That's what people do in a library.'

'I need your help with something.'

'Why do you think I would help y–'

'SHHHHHHHHHH!'

Mr Grindle was at the end of the row again, with a

thunderous expression. I pointed accusingly at Cal, who narrowed his eyes at me. I waited until Mr Grindle went back to his desk.

'Can we go somewhere where we can talk? Please? It's important.'

Cal sighed before reluctantly shutting the book. 'Fine.'

'*A History of London and its Buildings,*' I read aloud from the book's cover as we walked towards the front desk. 'Well, that sounds like the most boring book of all time. Is it by that Nicholas Huntley writer you're creepily obsessed with?'

'No. His book is about tanks.'

'Oh yeah. That other really interesting topic. Why would you bother reading a book about London's buildings? Why don't you just go around and look at them?'

'Because it's interesting to learn about their history and architectural detail,' Cal huffed, filling in a form for Mr Grindle, who was still staring at me dubiously. 'The Royale is mentioned in this, you know.'

'Why?'

'Because the hotel is an important historical building with incredibly intricate architecture,' Cal explained, looking at me as though I was mad.

'Well, duh, you can see that just by standing in the lobby with all its gold archways and the paintings and stuff. You don't need to waste your time reading that old thing.'

Going out of the library, I saw a particularly giggly Ella and Olly talking to each other nearby. Before they could see us, I quickly grabbed Cal's arm and pulled him sideways into the nearest doorway, which turned out to be a cleaning cupboard.

'Why are we in here?' he asked, accidentally kicking over a mop as I squeezed in next to him.

'Because we can get some privacy.' I shrugged, trying to act as though this was all planned.

'Sure.' He sighed. 'And it has nothing to do with you not wanting your friends to see you with me?'

'Don't be ridiculous.'

'Why don't you just tell me why you need my help so we can get this over with?'

'I'm here to offer you a proposition. You need a topic for your stupid journalism competition thing, right? What if I told you I had the best topic, which would guarantee you winning the top prize? Even better than Prince Gustav.'

Cal snorted. 'I'd be very surprised.'

'Trust me, you'll want to hear me out,' I insisted.

'Go on, then.'

I took a deep breath. 'An exclusive interview with the biggest pop star in the whole world, Skylar Chase.'

He looked impressed. 'You're serious?'

'Yes.' I nodded. 'There's no way anyone else in your stupid competition is going to get access to that kind of public figure, is there?'

'And Skylar Chase told you she would let me interview her?' he asked, looking doubtful.

'I haven't asked her yet, but we're friends,' I added hurriedly when he raised his eyebrows, 'she'll say yes, I'm sure of it.'

'OK, so what's the catch?'

I took a deep breath. 'You may remember that I went to a fashion show on Friday . . .'

'Yes, I remember trying to stop you and you not listening and then getting in loads of trouble. Like I predicted.' He folded his arms.

'That's the one.' I nodded. 'Well, Mum is now saying I can't go to the Christmas Ball.'

'Woe is you.'

'I know, right? Mum doesn't think I'm responsible. I have to persuade her that I am. Then she'll let me go.'

'And you think I can help you with that?'

'Yes.'

'Sorry to disappoint, but I'm not the right person to persuade her otherwise. I happen to completely agree with her.'

'I don't want you to talk to her. I want you to show me the ropes of the hotel.'

He blinked at me. 'What?'

'The hotel. I need you to show me how it all works. Who does what and when. What makes the hotel tick, blah blah blah. You know, all the boring stuff.'

'I'm sorry –' he shook his head – 'I'm confused.'

'OK, it's really not that hard to understand. Mum thinks that I don't care about responsibilities and the hotel and –'

'You don't,' he interrupted.

'Right, because I'm a *normal* teenager.' I was beginning to get impatient. This had better be worth all the hard work. 'But I'm going to learn to. Audrey is too busy to help me and she said you're the next best person to ask. You know how the hotel works and you know everyone, and she said you'd make sure we didn't get in anyone's way. Plus, you have nothing better to do.'

'What makes you think that?' he said defensively.

'Because you have no friends and you just sit around with your dad all day.'

'That's it.' He went to push open the door of the cupboard.

'Wait, wait, I'm sorry!' I said hurriedly, stopping him. 'That sounded bad. What I meant was, you're . . . uh . . .

passionate about the hotel. Look, you even read books about its architecture and stuff.'

'I can't believe I'm bothering to listen to you.'

'Cal, I wouldn't ask for your help if I wasn't desperate,' I whined. 'All you have to do is spend a few evenings and weekends teaching me how it all works.'

'No small task with your attention span.'

'I know you love a challenge,' I said hopefully. 'And in return, you'll get an interview with Skylar Chase. Most proper journalists don't get that opportunity. And I have to prove to Mum that I've made the effort to learn about the hotel.'

'Why are you so desperate to go to the Christmas Ball?'

'It's my favourite time of year. You know I love it.'

'Yeah, but right now you're telling me you're willing to actually do some work around the hotel and spend your free time learning things, which isn't really your style. So why are you *this* desperate to go?'

I shuffled my feet, knocking over a basket of bleach bottles.

'Ethan Duke asked me to go with him. You know. Like a date. And I can't cancel on *Ethan Duke.*' I bit my lip. 'So? Will you help me?'

I gripped his arm gently as he didn't respond. 'Cal? Pleeeeeeeeease?'

I gave him the biggest puppy eyes I could muster.

'Fine.' He sighed grudgingly. 'Stop looking at me like that. You'll damage your eye sockets.'

'YES!' I whooped. 'Thank you. You won't regret it.'

'Wanna bet?'

'When do we start?' I asked eagerly.

'We need to ask all the different team managers when it suits them for us to shadow,' Cal informed me. 'I'll let you know when I've sorted a plan.'

'Cool. Great idea. I'm excited to . . . you know . . . get to work.'

'Right, I'm sure,' he said, shaking his head. 'Let's get out of here.'

I followed him back out into the corridor at the exact moment Mr Grindle happened to be walking past from the library. He stopped in his tracks and observed us emerging with a stunned expression on his face.

'Trust me, Mr Grindle.' Cal sighed, walking past him. 'You really don't want to know.'

THIRTEEN

'No, not this one.'

Cal and Amy, one of the housekeeping staff, shared a glance.

'What do you mean?' Cal asked.

'Can't we do another room?'

'No,' Cal answered. 'Amy needs to do this room, so this is the one we're helping her with. What's wrong with the Sapphire Suite?'

'Ohhh,' Amy said, her eyes widening in understanding. 'This was Prince Gustav's room.'

Cal laughed and put his hand out for her to pass him the heavy, old-fashioned room key.

'Come on, Flick, it's not like it's haunted.'

He was still chuckling to himself as we walked through into the large suite. I shuddered at the memory of the last time I'd been here, when those burly security men had dragged me out.

'Want me to go and get your selfie stick so you can vlog about this moving experience to your millions of followers?' Cal asked, chucking the keys on the dressing table.

'Whatever,' I huffed, glaring at him. 'I can't vlog now I'm grounded, can I? Vloggers are meant to have interesting, glamorous lives. I'm stuck in here with you.'

'So grateful,' he murmured, sharing a look with Amy.

I settled myself on the sofa and kicked off my shoes as Amy began to unload the pile of linen from her trolley and on to the bed.

'What do you think you're doing?' Cal asked me. 'You need to help Amy with the sheets.'

It was only the first day of him showing me the ropes and I already felt VERY tired of the whole thing. It was also obvious that he was revelling in the opportunity to boss me about.

Cal had thought it a good idea to start my 'Royale education', as he pompously put it, with the housekeeping team on Saturday morning, so I could learn how everything looks so perfect all the time. He introduced me to Amy, who told me she'd worked at the hotel for three years, which was weird as I'd never noticed her before, and then we'd spent ages in the laundry room while Amy yapped on about her daily routine at Cal's request. I had stuck it out even though the laundry had an overpowering lavender smell, and I even managed to only yawn once the whole time she was talking, which was wildly impressive considering the topic.

I didn't really think it was necessary to shadow her for the rest of the afternoon, when I'd already heard what she did in way too much detail, but Cal insisted that doing the job myself would be the only way I could really learn about it. All I did was roll my eyes when he said that and he went off on one, saying this was my idea in the first place and that I wasn't going to impress my mum with that attitude. I went, 'Calm down, Grandpa,' and that just made him *more* annoyed and he made me push the stupid linen trolley the whole way to the room, which was really difficult because it had a dodgy wheel. It did however give me an excellent excuse when I accidentally-on-purpose rolled it sharply into the back of his ankle.

'Amy, I think you've made a mistake,' I pointed out, lifting one of the folded sheets off the pile as she stripped the bed. 'There's only one bed in here but you've put out enough linen to do the whole hotel.'

She smiled, as she shook the pillows out of their cases. 'No, that's all just for one bed. There are a lot of layers involved. Right, shake out the bottom sheet.'

'Which one's the bottom one?' I asked. 'They all look identical.'

'Not at all, some of them are patterned,' she said,

coming over to show me. 'You see this detailed stitching here in the corners?'

'Oh yeah.' I looked closer. 'That's quite pretty.'

'They're specially made for the hotel,' she told me proudly. 'You can't buy these sheets. This one is the bottom one.' She threw a sheet at me. 'Shake it out and then lift it across the bed and grab the corners. I'll help with the other side.'

Doing what I was told, I shook the folded sheet and then, taking two corners, I waved it up above my head so it would open up and spread out across the bed, perhaps a bit too enthusiastically. As I threw it up in the air, I accidentally let go of the corners I was holding, and it floated down over my head. It was so big that I tried to find my way out, but somehow managed to tread on it and get stuck.

'Are you pretending to be a ghost?' I heard Cal ask, as I started pulling it forwards over my head and face to see if that would work.

'No,' I replied, breathing in a mouthful of the sheet.

'Have you never made a bed before? Seriously, what are you doing?'

'What is wrong with this thing?' I said, thrashing my arms about and ignoring Amy's giggles. 'Why doesn't it have an end to it?'

'You're standing on it, you numpty.' Cal laughed.

'Get off it and then just pull it over your head.'

'Who uses the word "numpty"?' I retorted. 'You are such a –'

Unfortunately, I didn't get to finish the end of my sentence because, in trying to get the sheet out from under my feet, my socks slipped as I pulled it forwards and I completely lost my balance, stumbling backwards and falling flat across the bed, wrapped up in the sheet like an Egyptian mummy.

Cal was never going to let me live this one down.

They both burst into hysterical laughter and when Amy came to my aid, pulling the sheet off me, I saw that Cal was bent over double, clutching his stomach.

'I'm sorry,' he wheezed, as I threw him a dirty look. 'But you should have seen yourself scrabbling about under there!'

'I'm sure it was hilarious,' I huffed, going into the bathroom to sort out my hair.

When I came back through, Amy fanned the sheet perfectly over the bed with barely a flick of her wrists and pulled the corners under the mattress in less than a minute.

'How did you do that?' I asked her, putting my hands on my hips. 'There must be a trick to it, which you're not telling me.'

'Practice,' she answered simply, fiddling with yet more sheets for the top layers.

'How did you get it so smooth?' I said, running my hand across the mattress.

'We iron them.'

My mouth fell open. 'You iron the bed sheets?'

'Of course.'

'All of them?'

'Yes.'

I stared at her and Cal came to stand next to me as Amy got the gold patterned bedspread ready to lay out for the finishing touch.

'Amazing, isn't it?' he said, helping her by stretching out the corner of the bedspread on our side. 'Amy makes it look easy.' She smiled at him gratefully.

I hated to agree with Cal Weston but I had to nod. There are hundreds of rooms in the hotel, including twin and family rooms and if each bed had this many sheets on it . . . well, that is more ironing than I could imagine. I watched as Amy swiftly arranged the pillows and gold cushions into a perfect arc across the bed.

I never thought I'd be so impressed by someone just making a bed. Hanging out with Cal was clearly turning me into a loser.

'Time to clean the bathroom,' Amy said, grabbing the

bucket of cleaning products from the bottom of the trolley and opening the door to the en suite.

'No way,' I said, shaking my head as Cal gave me a knowing look. 'No chance.'

'How do you think they look so squeaky clean the whole time?' he said, pushing me towards it. 'Someone has to do it.'

'Why don't you empty the bins?' Amy suggested as she folded the corner of the toilet roll into a triangle and popped it on to the holder. 'That would be a great help.'

'Good idea,' Cal said brightly, searching through the trolley for two pairs of latex gloves. 'Put these on,' he instructed me.

'What do you mean "empty the bins"? Where?' I asked, taking the gloves and inspecting them.

Cal snorted. 'You've never emptied the bins? Doesn't your mum ever ask you?'

'No.' I shrugged. 'I don't even know if *she* does them. They just get emptied.'

'You are unbelievable,' he said, lifting the bag out of the bin under the dressing table and tying the ends, before holding it out at me.

I stared at it in horror.

'Come on, put the gloves on,' he encouraged. 'If you're

going to be in charge one day, you have to know this place, inside out.'

I reluctantly pulled on the gloves and took the bin bag, holding my nose. 'Ew.'

'It is NOT that bad,' he said, leading the way out of the room.

He picked up a few more bin bags put out by another member of staff, who was cleaning the rooms further down the corridor. He yelled thanks to Cal as he passed them to me and we got in the lift.

'How come you know everyone?' I asked, holding the bin bags at arm's length away from me.

'Because I bother to talk to them,' he said pointedly.

We went out the exit next to the laundry room and Cal gestured to the big industrial bins. I put the bags down on the floor and, one by one, threw them into the bigger bin.

'Eugh,' I yelped, as I missed and hit the edge of the bin, causing the bag I was holding to explode. I looked at the mess scattered around our feet. 'Who do we get to clean this up?'

He raised his eyebrows. 'Guess.'

'Nooooo!' I cried.

'You're wearing gloves,' he said, pinging the bottom of his for effect. 'Come on, I'll help you.'

He bent down and began to gather up the rubbish,

every now and then straightening up to throw it in the bin. He watched me in bemusement as I gracefully bent my knees to join him, whimpering the whole way down.

'We'll be done in no time,' he said. 'Just be careful of the mice. Look, there's one by your shoe.'

'WHAT?'

I screamed and leaped to my feet, running away from the bin and slamming myself against the wall, looking around the concrete madly. 'WHERE HAS IT GONE? WHERE IS IT?'

'I'm joking! I'm joking!' He laughed, standing up. 'I swear, it was just a joke. There's no mouse!'

'That was NOT funny!' I yelled. 'You gave me a heart attack!'

'I'm sorry.' He chuckled. 'You should have seen your face!'

I came back over and couldn't help but smile in relief. I guess that may have been a slight overreaction. I giggled as I bent down to pick up the last bits of rubbish.

'Whoa,' Cal said, his eyes twinkling. 'Did you just *laugh*?'

'So?'

'I don't think I've seen you laugh in years.'

'Well, maybe that's because you're not very funny.'

'Touché.' He grinned. 'I forgot you had a sense of

humour. Hard to notice it these days under all those airs and graces.'

I straightened up, holding a banana skin.

'I think my sense of humour would really enjoy throwing this banana skin in that smug face of yours,' I said, as he took a small step back.

'Put that in the bin, Flick.' He gulped. 'You know I hate bananas.'

'That didn't stop you leaving that fake snake in my locker when you knew I hated snakes.'

'That was different.' He shivered as I dangled the banana skin in front of him threateningly. 'That was years ago. And it wasn't unhygienic.' His eyes shifted from the banana skin to meet mine. He couldn't suppress a grin. 'And it was hilarious. You screamed so loudly.'

Big mistake. And he knew it.

I began to chase him around the bins gleefully, as he begged me through nervous laughter to put the banana skin down. I waited until I was close enough and then launched it with perfect aim, hitting him in the back of his head.

'FLICK!'

'You should be grateful I didn't get you in the face.' I laughed, as Cal desperately wiped flecks of banana from his hair.

A polite cough came from the doorway and we looked up to see Amy smiling at us.

'When you're ready, we have several more rooms to do,' she said, tapping her watch and disappearing back inside.

We peeled off our gloves and tossed them into the bin before following Amy, whereupon she proceeded to tell me all about the different types of bacteria found in a bathroom.

This year's Christmas Ball had better be good.

Hey Flick, it's Ethan. I got your number from Sky, hope that's OK. When are you free for the vlog?

Hey! That would be amazing! Um, I'm grounded forever, so it would have to be in a few weeks. Unless you came to the hotel and we recorded it here? X

Cool. Will let you know

Hey Grace, are you busy?

Hey! No, not busy. Watching a film with Olly. It's boring. He always gets to pick

Can I ask you something? If a guy texts you but doesn't put any kisses at the end . . . do you think that's important? Just out of interest

HAS ETHAN DUKE TEXTED YOU? OMG OMG OMG OMG OMG OMG

Grace. Focus

Right. Sure. Um, no I don't think that really means anything. Olly never puts any kisses at the end of his texts

Yeah but he's your brother

That's a good point. You want me to ask him if he puts kisses at the end of his texts to other people?

NO

Oh. OK. I won't ask him

You've asked him, haven't you

No

ꙮ ♡ ✳

Who's texting you and not putting kisses at the end?

Who is this?

Olly. Hey

I don't know what you're talking about

I think it's not really a big deal

OK

Are you embarrassed?

Nope

Don't be embarrassed

I'm not

Great talking to you

Grace is dead to me

180

FOURTEEN

Ella was driving me nuts.

Since her party, she hadn't SHUT UP about Olly and his 'amazing dark eyes and long delicate eyelashes' for one second. Delicate? *Really?* If anyone else in our group used that word to describe their boyfriend's eyelashes, Ella would scrap them right off her sleepover guest list.

He was, she reminded us at every possible moment, the best-looking boy in the whole school. And, yeah, I'm not going to say Olly is bad-looking because, let's face it, he wouldn't look out of place standing next to One Direction and I was happy to note that he had moved on from sleeveless vests for his band performances, and was sporting more tasteful T-shirts that still did a good job of showing off his muscly arms. But it's not like he's Ethan Duke. I was actually looking forward to not seeing Ella during half-term next week and getting a break from her and her gooey stories.

'She's being so selfish,' I complained to Grace as we strolled towards the cafeteria together one lunchtime.

'She hasn't asked me one question about Ethan or Sky and, no offence, they're more interesting than your brother.'

'Why don't you just tell her you want to talk about them?' Grace offered, going through the lunch trays and passing me a dry one.

'I can't do that. She should *want* to know.'

'I think her brain is a bit fogged up at the moment with Olly.' She pulled a face. 'He's all she talks about.'

'There they are now.' I sighed, gesturing to a table in the middle of the room where Olly was talking enthusiastically to the friend opposite him, while Ella sat next to him listening patiently. 'Do they ever spend a second apart?'

'Actually,' Grace began, coming to stand next to me and look over at their cringe display, 'he was saying that he finds her a bit . . . much.'

'Really?'

'Yeah, he said he wished he had got to know her a bit more before you know –' she grimaced – 'all the smooching.'

'Don't use the word "smooching", Grace. People might hear you.'

'Sorry. Don't tell Ella,' she pleaded.

'I won't, she'd never let you sit at her table if she knew

you called it "smooching". You're lucky I'm so lenient.'

'I mean, about what Olly said. I don't want her to hate me.'

'She wouldn't hate you, Grace,' I said impatiently, taking a plate of lasagne. 'It's not you who said it, it's Olly.'

'Yeah, but I think he's the only reason she's friends with me.'

I tore my eyes away from Ella stroking Olly's arm and looked curiously at Grace. She was obviously right. But I didn't know she *knew* that.

'It's OK,' she said quietly. 'I don't really mind.'

She suddenly looked very small and hunched, and I felt a wave of sympathy for her. Ella had a way of making people feel very small, especially people like Grace who just let her walk all over them.

'You should mind,' I heard myself saying. 'You should have more confidence. Stand up for yourself a bit.'

'I know.' She nodded, but she said it in a way that didn't sound like she believed it.

'Look,' I began sternly, 'she wouldn't keep hanging out with you if she didn't like you.'

It was a lie, but at least it would stop her from looking so sad.

'You think?' She blinked up at me gratefully.

'Yeah. Now, let's go. I'm starving.'

She followed me across the cafeteria and we slid our trays on to Ella and Olly's table. They all looked up to say hey when Grace and I sat down, before Olly and his friend, Liam, returned to their heated debate about a book I hadn't read, while Ella concentrated on lapping up every word that came out of Olly's mouth. I let my mind dreamily drift off to Ethan and appearing on his vlog, which annoyingly sparked a string of nervous thoughts, thanks to something stupid Cal had said.

I hadn't told him about appearing on Ethan's vlog on purpose. He had overheard the conversation I was having with Matthew and Fritz, and had found the whole concept hilarious.

'What is so funny?' I'd said grumpily, as he came round the back of the reception desk, where I was sitting with Fritz on my lap. The silver tag had fallen off his favourite collar and I had taken it to Matthew to see if it was fixable or if I'd have to ring up Tiffany's and ask them to send him another.

'You going on Ethan Duke's vlog,' Cal said, rummaging through his bag, which he'd left with his dad behind the counter, and pulling out a bag of crisps.

'I think it sounds interesting,' Matthew said, fiddling with the delicate clasp of the dog tag.

'Thank you, Matthew,' I replied, tickling Fritz's belly

until he heard the rustle of the crisp bag and flew off my lap to go and paw innocently at Cal's leg.

'What are you going to talk about? How you can't even make a bed without getting stuck in the sheets?' Cal asked, shoving several crisps into his mouth at one time, ignoring the pool of drool from Fritz forming at his feet.

'I will be talking about my life.'

'Aren't you saving that intriguing topic of conversation for your own vlogs, which are yet to make an appearance?' Cal snorted.

I narrowed my eyes at him as Matthew smiled to himself.

'I'll use Ethan's vlog appearance to launch my OWN vlog. It will be like . . . a teaser.'

Cal let out a loud 'HA' causing bits of crisp to fly everywhere.

'Ew! Matthew, look! We'll have to bleach the desk now.'

Matthew sighed. 'Go and eat those somewhere else, please, Callum.'

'Yes, *Callum*,' I sneered.

'Fine by me.' He smiled, offering Fritz a crisp and almost losing his fingers in the process.

'When are you going to train this mutt?'

'He's perfectly trained,' I said defensively, as Fritz took

Cal's shoelaces in his feet and started pulling them. 'And don't call him a mutt.'

'He's the worst-trained dog I've ever met.'

'And you're an expert, are you?' I folded my arms. Cal scrunched up his empty crisp packet, lobbed it into the bin and then picked up Fritz and tickled his chin.

'I might not be an expert, but I do know that dogs shouldn't pee behind the reception desk.'

Matthew's head jerked up.

'WHAT?'

'*Cal!*' I hissed.

'See you guys later,' Cal laughed, grabbing his bag and dropping Fritz into my lap as he breezed out of the reception hall and through the hotel doors.

After about five minutes of explaining to Matthew that it had only happened on one occasion, when Fritz was a puppy, I was let off the hook and allowed to escape back to my room, where I spent the next few hours googling Ethan Duke and going through all his videos. Cal's stupid comments had made me feel a bit nervous about what I was actually going to talk about, so I wanted to check the vibe of other guests. Most of them were able to talk about their recent films or music releases. What was I going to say?

Would announcing the launch of my vlogging channel be an interesting enough topic? Would Ethan find me as much of a laughing stock as Cal did? And what was I going to talk about on my own vlogs anyway? I wasn't sure I'd thought this whole thing through. All these thoughts were starting to give me a headache.

Who knew that vlogging was such hard work?

'She really is in her own world. Flick? Helloooooooo.'

I broke out of my daze and saw everyone around the table watching me expectantly.

'Welcome back to Earth.' Olly laughed. 'Penny for your thoughts?'

'I was just telling everyone about how, on the last Saturday of half-term, my parents are taking me for a really posh lunch,' Ella boasted, before I had the chance to answer Olly, 'and then I'm going to Olly's house in the evening.'

'Everyone's invited,' Olly added.

'Our parents have set up a projector in the basement,' Grace enthused. 'And we've made it really cosy in there, so we're going to have a movie night.'

'I'm going to do the popcorn challenge,' Liam said proudly. 'How much popcorn I can fit in my mouth at once. Got to beat Tom's record.'

'Sounds . . . interesting.'

'Are you going to come?' Olly asked.

'I can't, I'm still grounded.'

'That sucks.' Everyone else nodded in agreement with him.

'It's OK.' I shrugged, seizing an opportunity. 'I need to prepare for Ethan's vlog.'

Grace dropped her fork with a clang. 'What?'

'Oh,' I said innocently. 'Didn't I tell you? Ethan's asked me to do a guest vlog.'

Whispers of excitement satisfactorily spread down the table. Of course, Ella then had to go and open her big mouth and ruin it all.

'*You?*' She laughed. 'But why would you be on Ethan Duke's vlog?'

'Why wouldn't she be on it?' Olly enquired, catching my eye.

'I just mean, what would she talk about?' Ella said, flustered, dropping her hand from where it had been permanently resting on his arm. 'It's not like she's famous.'

'She's been on all the fashion websites since the Lewis Blume show,' Grace said hurriedly.

My stomach tightened at Ella's sharp words. Would everyone else think that? But if Ethan thinks I'm good enough then it doesn't matter – he knows what he's talking about so who cares what Ella says?

Except, I hadn't heard from Ethan in a few days. Maybe

he had changed his mind and he didn't want me on it any more and now the whole school would know that he had dropped me . . .

'It's not a big deal, just a bit of fun,' I said, standing up quickly before anyone could say anything else. 'Anyway, I'm sad to miss out on the popcorn challenge.'

'Right on.' Liam nodded, holding up his hand for me to high-five. 'It will be epic.'

'Where are you going?' Grace asked.

'I've got to make a phone call,' I lied, shoving my tray on the rack. 'I'll see you in a bit.'

I got outside, wrapped my coat tighter around me and sat down on a bench, looking out across the schoolyard – thanks to the cold weather, I had the place to myself. I turned my phone off and on again, to check that my messages weren't playing up and Ethan hadn't been texting me all this time begging me to let him know when we could schedule in a date for filming. I stared at it as the home screen refreshed. No new messages.

After a few minutes of pretending not to be cold, I admitted to myself that my hands were about to fall off and I should head back inside. I heard footsteps behind me and thought that maybe Ella had come to apologise for saying that I wasn't famous enough to be on the vlog. I got ready with my superior 'I-may-or-may-not-forgive-

189

you' face. But it wasn't her.

'You all right?'

I spun round to see Olly, hunched over in the cold with his hands shoved in his pockets. He came to sit down next to me.

'Yeah, I'm fine.' I held up my phone. 'Just finished my call so was about to come inside.'

'Who was it?'

'Oh . . . Ethan Duke. Yeah. We were brainstorming some ideas.'

'I just wanted to come out here and check . . .' He paused and met my eyes with his. 'I wanted to make sure you weren't upset about what Ella said. About the famous thing.'

I laughed, a little more high-pitched than normal. 'Pah! I'm not upset.'

He raised his eyebrows. 'You went a bit pale when she said it.'

'No I didn't. I don't care. She's just jealous, as usual.'

'Well, I'm glad you're OK,' he said, cupping his hands together and breathing into them.

We sat in silence until I felt a bit uncomfortable. It felt as though he had something more to say and, considering it was really cold and I'd already spent ages out here pretending to be on the phone, I thought I'd help him out and cut to the chase.

'Did you come out here to ask me if I'll ask Ethan to have your band on his vlog or something? Because I don't think that he –'

'What?' Olly looked taken aback. 'No. I came out to check you were all right.'

'Oh. Right, it just seemed like –'

'Whatever, I'll leave you to it.' He stood up abruptly and stomped back towards school.

If anyone else had been so touchy and stormed off over a tiny comment like that, I would have left them to get over themselves, but Olly had defended me at lunch when his girlfriend had taken a swipe at me, so I thought I should probably catch up with him and make amends. Boys are so high maintenance.

'Sorry.' I tried to catch his eye as I fell into step with him but he was staring straight ahead.

'It's OK,' he said sharply.

'I thought –'

'I know what you thought,' he interrupted, stopping at the door and turning to look me straight in the eye. 'Don't you think it's a bit sad that when someone is trying to be nice, you think that they want something from you?'

I opened my mouth to reply but the door swung open and a load of sixth-form girls huddled out, breaking us apart, and when they spotted me they launched into a bunch of questions about Lewis Blume's fashion show, blocking Olly from view. When I was finally able to grapple my way through them back into the warmth, he had gone inside and was standing with Ella, Grace and Liam, staring at his feet, while the others laughed politely at something Ella was droning on about.

As I got close to them, I felt a tap on my shoulder and turned to see Cal standing in front of me, his headphones round his neck and a pile of books in his arms. It was literally like he went *out of his way* to look like a stereotypical nerd.

'What?' I asked, maybe a little harsher than I should have. Ella fell silent and, even though I had my back turned to the group, I knew they were watching.

'I just wanted to check we were still on for Saturday.'

I glanced over my shoulder. Ella looked repulsed. Yep, they had heard.

'Yes, fine. See you then,' I whispered, trying to tell him to go away with my eyes.

His eyes drifted over my shoulder to our judging audience, and a mischievous grin formed on his face. I'd seen that look before many times. Right before he played a big joke on someone.

Oh no.

'I'm SO looking forward to our date, babe,' he said loudly enough for the whole corridor to stop what they were doing and look at us. I froze in shock while he lifted his headphones back over his ears, winked at me and sauntered off down the hall.

Ella's mouth dropped open. '*What* did Cal Weston just say to you?'

> **Remind me to kill you on Saturday**

Good evening to you too

> **WHY DID YOU SAY THAT?**

Say what?

> **Everyone is going to think we're dating!**
> **We are NOT dating!**

Honey, you're breaking my heart

> **You need to fix this**

Fix what? Your sense of humour?

THIS IS NOT FUNNY

Typical hothead. It's not a big deal.
Gotta go. Talk later

What?! NO, you can't go!
I'm not done with you yet!

Don't you ever get bored of whining?
How long is this going to take?

As long as it takes for you to
tell the whole school that we
are not dating and this was all just
a stupid joke

You want me to go round to
each person at school, ask them
if they think me and you are dating
and if they say yes you want me to
then tell them that they're wrong?

Yes, great idea. That would be perfect

Dream on, Royale

Just send an email round! Hack into the school database and get everyone's email addresses. Then you can message everyone in one go

What makes you think I can just hack into the school database??

Because you are a nerd and that's the sort of thing nerds know how to do

I guess I could . . .

YES! Thank you

Oh no wait, I'm busy. Gotta go

NO! CAL. COME BACK HERE. SEND THE EMAIL

Nope

WHY NOT?

Because you haven't said the magic word

HOW OLD ARE YOU?

One magic word and you get your way

OK FINE. Cal, PLEASE can you send an email round telling everyone we're not dating? There, I said it

That's not the magic word

CAL

It's not and you know it

I'm not going to say it

You were the one who came up with it. I think it's adorable

WHY ARE YOU SO ANNOYING?

I think you secretly find me endearing

EUGH. Fine fine fine. I'll say the stupid magic word

I'm ready and waiting . . .

Poopdopalopolis

The whole sentence please

Cal, can you send an email to everyone poopdopalopolis?

Bad news: I can't hack into the school database and send an email. Good news: I just took a screenshot of you saying 'poopdopalopolis'. I love our chats

I hate you

FIFTEEN

On the first Saturday of half-term, the doorbell of our flat rang at 7 a.m.

Mum answered because she had already been up for a couple of hours – as she likes to tell everyone who will listen, she's an 'early bird' who apparently doesn't need to sleep like normal human beings.

'Flick?' she said softly, coming through my door while knocking, which is one of my pet hates about her because WHAT is the point of knocking if you're just barging on in anyway?

I mumbled at her to go away and then turned over, snuggling down into my cosy duvet.

Mum and I were back on speaking terms, not that it made a huge amount of difference considering how busy she was in the lead-up to Christmas. She was constantly dashing off to meetings at the moment, and then rushing back in the evenings to change her heels into other, higher heels because she had to go to a dinner or party somewhere across London with a load of boring, important people. The Christmas Ball was also always on her mind – she kept repeating her orders and triple-checking the guest list. Even Matthew had told her to 'chill on out' – which he could not pull off, by the way, and once again displays the cringe-worthy gene pool from which Cal was produced.

Still, her mood had definitely improved. I knew that things had taken a turn for the better when she made a joke for the first time in weeks. A couple of days ago, I had heard down the hotel grapevine that the Editor of *GQ* had made a reservation for dinner, so I made sure Fritz was looking his most dapper in case we bumped into him. As Fritz came trotting out of my bedroom sporting his red velvet smoking jacket, Mum was coming through to the living room from her study reading an email on her phone. She stopped as he padded past her on the way to his bowl.

'Are you two sneaking off to a fashion show again?' she'd said, before returning to her email.

We may be friends again but she still hadn't said anything about the Christmas Ball. She can be so stubborn.

'Flick,' she repeated, moving over to my bed and shaking my shoulder.

I batted her away.

'You need to get up.'

'It's half-term,' I mumbled into my pillow. 'And a Saturday.'

'Cal's here.'

I slid my eye mask up on to my forehead. 'Huh?'

'Cal is here,' she said, nodding to the door. 'He's waiting for you in the living room.'

'Why?' I asked, rubbing my eyes.

Her eyes sparkled with curiosity. 'He said that you've got a date.'

I groaned and sat up as she waited, perched neatly on my bed.

'So?' she prompted, as I reached for the clock. 'What does he mean, a date? Are you guys . . . *seeing* each other or something?'

'EW, MUM!' I threw my pillow at her. 'He just said that to annoy me!'

'All right, all right.' She laughed, standing and holding up her hands. 'I was just asking.'

'Well, don't ask in the future,' I huffed. Then I saw the clock. 'What the – You have GOT to be joking! Is that really the time?'

I reached for my duvet and lay back down, pulling it over my head, but Mum just pulled it straight back off again.

'It's rude to keep guests waiting. Come on, up you get.'

'I don't believe this,' I grumbled, pulling on my dressing gown and stomping out into the living room where Cal was sitting comfortably on the sofa, typing on his laptop. Mum left us to it and went to the kitchen to put the kettle on, followed by a lively Fritz, excited for his breakfast.

'Morning, sunshine.' He glanced up and then returned to his typing with a small smile. 'Your hair looks pretty.'

I felt the back of my head where it was all sticking up and narrowed my eyes at him.

'Well then?' I said, tapping my foot.

'Well then, what?' he said, without looking up.

'What are you doing here? It's 7 a.m.!'

'I told you, we're helping Chef in the kitchen today.'

Mum came through from the kitchen holding a tray of mugs. 'You're doing what?'

'Helping Chef in the kitchen.' Cal smiled, gratefully taking a cup of coffee from her. 'Flick is keen to learn his routine. And to improve her cooking.'

Mum stared at me in disbelief. '*Really?*'

'It's 7 in the morning!' I repeated, ignoring my mum's questioning looks.

'Yeah, so you better hurry up or you're going to miss breakfast prep. We're already later than planned. Chef's been there ages.' He took a satisfied sip of his coffee.

'This is delicious, Christine. Just what we need before our day of fun in the kitchen.'

'Why, thank you, Callum.' She smiled. 'How wonderful that you're spending the day with Chef.' She passed me a coffee. 'I'm really impressed.'

Cal looked very pleased with himself as Mum went back into her study.

'You're welcome,' he whispered.

'Can you PLEASE stop telling people we are dating?' I hissed back. 'First the entire school, and now my mum. Are you purposefully trying to bug me?'

A wide smile spread across his face. 'Is that a trick question?'

I stuck my tongue out at him and then locked myself in the bathroom to shower and get ready. Just as I was pulling my trainers on in the living room, a text came through from Sky.

> What are you up to today?
> I have the day off and want
> a break from your country's
> persistent reporters. Spa day?

Aha! Perfect timing. Although, seriously, does no one sleep around here?

'Sky wants to hang out so it looks like I'll have to take a rain check on the kitchen,' I said chirpily.

'No way.' Cal laughed. 'That's what got you in trouble in the first place. You can't just drop everything for Skylar Chase. Say you're busy. She'll understand and I'm sure she won't be heartbroken at missing your company.'

'But –'

'No buts,' Cal said sternly. 'It was generous of Chef to allow us to shadow him for the day. We're not cancelling. And if you try to escape then our deal is off and you can kiss goodbye to Ethan Duke and the Christmas Ball. Didn't you hear what your mum said? She's genuinely impressed with you. Your plan is working.'

I sighed. There was nothing worse than Cal Weston being right.

Hey, would have loved to but I'm helping out in the kitchen today. I'm so sorry!

Sounds fun! Can I join?

'I guess we can ask Chef,' Cal said, when I showed him the message, looking as surprised as I felt at her question. Of all the things in London that a famous pop star could do on a day off, hanging out with two younger teenagers

203

in a hotel kitchen was a peculiar option. But, then again, Skylar Chase wasn't your average pop star.

When we got to the kitchen, I couldn't believe how busy it was. Everywhere you looked, someone was cooking, preparing any kind of breakfast food you can think of, from bacon and eggs, to pastries and fresh fruit salads. I waved at Sasha who was whisking scrambled eggs by one of the stoves. She grinned broadly at me.

'Right, my pretties,' Chef said, bustling over to us and moving us out of the way of the immaculately dressed waiters who were coming in to take trays of food up into the dining room. 'You stand over here and watch the magic happen.'

'How long have you been here?' I asked, taking in all the activity.

'A while,' Chef said, patting one of his cooks on the back as we passed him arranging almonds on a croissant with great precision.

'And it's like this every day?'

'Yes, of course.' He put his hands on his hips. 'How do you think breakfast gets on the table? By elves?'

'I just didn't really think about it.'

'And why doesn't that surprise me?' he said, sharing a knowing look with Cal. 'The menus take a lot of hard work. I have to create new dishes, search for the right suppliers, hunt down the perfect produce.' Chef smiled. 'I love it, of course.'

'You don't just have a set menu?' I asked, watching one of his cooks slide some poached eggs so cautiously on to a plate, you'd think he was handling priceless diamonds.

'It changes day to day –'

'Day to day?' I repeated, astonished.

'Of course.' Chef shrugged, as though that was normal. 'The menu is seasonal so it depends on what we have each day. We have a few staple dishes but sometimes the catch isn't what we were expecting –'

'Catch?'

'Fish,' Cal explained, sneaking a pastry.

'So,' I said slowly, working this all out in my brain, 'the fisherman might not have caught the right fish?'

'In which case, the menu changes and I can add a dish or come up with a new recipe depending on what he has caught.' Chef nodded.

'Isn't that difficult?'

Chef's eyes lit up. 'Absolutely! But I love coming up with new recipes; that is my passion. I like a challenge.'

'Chef gets his inspiration from everywhere,' Cal added. 'He's been inspired by people, music and sometimes even architecture.'

'He's right,' Chef insisted, when I shook my head in disbelief.

'Architecture can inspire . . . a new recipe? How is that even possible?'

Chef tapped the side of his head. 'Use your imagination. The structure, the shapes, the colours, the atmosphere the building creates. One of my favourite dishes was inspired by Westminster Abbey.'

'You see?' Cal smiled. 'The kitchen is a lot cooler than you think.'

I was almost impressed by the whole thing but then Cal had to go and say, 'The kitchen is a lot cooler than you think,' and ruin it. How he thinks it's acceptable to make these lame comments in public is beyond me.

'Of course, it's not about the kitchen itself.' Chef clapped his hands together. 'It's about the people in it.'

He began to point to various people around the kitchen, describing what each of their specialities was or what they were training to do, before claiming with a chuckle that he was going to test me on it later to check that I had been listening. Which would be unfair because there's no way I'd pass a test – not that I hadn't been listening, but because there were SO many members of his team and so many different components and departments to the kitchen.

I mean, one guy, Liam, was just in charge of the herbs. HERBS. That was Liam's job role, to look after all the herbs.

I only know the name of one herb.

'Really? Which one?' Cal laughed when I made that point to him. Chef had rushed off to taste test some hollandaise sauce, instructing Cal not to let me near the baking cupboard while we waited for him.

'Parsley.'

'That's it? Parsley? You seriously can't name any other herbs?'

'All right, Herb Guru, name some.'

'Coriander, basil, rosemary, sage, mint, thyme . . .'

'And this guy is in charge of all those?' I interrupted, pointing at Liam, who was tending to some weird sort of plant. 'Isn't that more like being a gardener than being a chef?'

'Not at all,' Chef corrected, returning and catching the end of our conversation. 'The right herb can transform a dish.'

'Flick has a lot to learn when it comes to cooking,' Cal informed him, stealing another croissant from a tray and taking a large bite.

'Excuse you, but I am an *excellent* cook!'

Here's the thing: I am a terrible cook. My brain cells

just don't seem to connect when it comes to the kitchen. I have tried to cook, like the time with the pizza, but I always get bored or distracted, so I figure it makes more sense to let other people cook for me and then the building won't get set on fire or anything.

I don't know what it is with Cal, but the way he says things always makes me want to argue with him. Maybe it's because he's always so sure of himself – I just want to prove him wrong, even if I actually have no idea.

Which is how I found myself announcing that I was an excellent cook to a kitchen full of professional chefs.

Cal put his croissant down and rubbed the pastry crumbs off his hands.

'You think you're an excellent cook?' he asked with a mocking smile.

You see what I'm talking about? Who wouldn't want to wipe that stupid smile off his face?

'Yes. I am.'

'OK then.'

'OK then, what?'

He gestured at the stove next to him. 'OK then, cook. We'd love to see your signature dish.'

I opened my mouth to explain that we didn't have time for cooking when we were supposed to be learning, but everyone suddenly fell silent and stopped what they were doing to stare at who had just walked into the kitchen.

Skylar Chase.

She came clacking across the floor to us in her very high heels, smiling at all the chefs as she passed. I'd asked Chef earlier if she could come join us and he'd given his approval, as well as offering me the unwelcome information that he often sang her songs in the shower.

'Hey,' she said cheerily, a wave of expensive perfume hitting me as she pulled me into a hug. 'It feels like ages.'

I pulled away to see Cal frozen to the spot, his mouth slightly open as he stared at her. Chef took off his hat and took her hand to kiss it.

'Miss Chase, what an honour to have you in my kitchen.'

'It's an honour to be here, thank you for letting me come see it,' she enthused, looking around her as all the kitchen staff stared in awe. One chef had paused midway through drizzling treacle over a pancake and the plate was now overflowing. Sky's eyes landed on Cal, who was frozen to the spot, and she fluttered her eyelashes at him.

'Hi, I'm Sky. You must be Cal. I've heard lots about you.'

Cal spluttered a hello, practically choking on his own spit and providing me with plenty of ammo should he ever feel the need to tease me about anything ever again. At least I didn't lose my mind in front of celebrities.

OK, fine, so there was that time when I shouted 'JAW' at Ethan Duke. But that's different.

Chef ordered one of the cooks to pull up a chair for Sky, and then told her that she was about to witness something spectacular.

'Flick is going to whip you up something. She is a self-professed *excellent* cook.'

Everyone's eyes turned to me.

'No, no, no. Surely Sky would rather you, the head chef of Hotel Royale,' I emphasised, 'cook her a delicious breakfast fit for royalty.'

'Nah, I'm happy for you to cook me something,' Sky said, sharing a mischievous smile with Chef. 'What's on the menu?'

I racked my brain for anything that I had ever made before. The list was short. I glanced back at the treacle now spreading in a pool across the work surface.

'Pancakes,' I squeaked. 'I can make you a pancake.'

'I love pancakes.' Sky laughed.

On instruction from Chef, Sasha hurried over with a frying pan and all the ingredients I'd need, lining them up neatly.

'Good luck!' she whispered as she placed down the bowl of flour.

'I need it!' I whispered back.

'No conferring with Sasha,' Cal said, finding his ability to talk again. 'And no googling the recipe. Pass me your phone so there's no cheating.'

I slapped my phone into his palm and then put on the apron that Sasha passed me. I hesitated at the next piece of apparel handed over.

'Really?' I asked Chef, dangling the hair net from my finger.

'Really.'

I rolled my eyes and then shoved it on my head, letting Sasha help me tuck in all the bits of hair round my face and looking daggers at Cal as he burst out laughing.

'It suits you,' Sky declared through giggles.

Ignoring the lot of them, I rolled up my sleeves and began to attempt a pancake, while the rest of the kitchen got back to work and Chef got back to bossing them all about. Regaining his composure, Cal started asking Sky about her latest album, leaving me to get on with it without the pressure of the two of them watching the process.

Miraculously, I remembered how to make the batter and couldn't help but feel extremely proud of myself as I poured some of it into the hot frying pan.

'Very impressive!' Sky cheered as I stood aside to let her and Cal admire it. 'Now, flip it.'

'Your wish is my command,' I said, grabbing the handle of the pan with both hands and tossing the pancake with gusto.

Unfortunately, it was a little bit too much gusto. The pancake flew high into the air, over my head and landed with a splat on Chef's head.

I gasped and Sky clapped her hand to her mouth. The whole kitchen froze as we waited for Chef's reaction.

'What?' he said finally, looking round at his staff. 'You guys don't like my new hat?'

We exploded into a fit of giggles and applause, as Chef did a twirl.

'I stand corrected,' Cal said, still laughing, 'you can cook . . . something.'

'Wow.' I put down the pan triumphantly. 'Did you just admit you were wrong? Has that ever happened in your entire life?'

'There's a first time for everything.'

'Looks like I'm going hungry.' Sky sighed, watching Chef remove the pancake from his head and throw it in the bin. 'I better go upstairs and get some breakfast in the dining room.'

'It will be the best breakfast you ever had!' Chef yelled across the kitchen, as Sky got ready to leave.

'I don't doubt it.' She smiled.

'It's been nice talking to you,' Cal said quickly. 'Hope the tour is a big success.'

'Thanks. Hey,' she said, flashing him a gleaming smile, 'you should come to my party if you're free. It's before I fly back to LA.'

Cal gulped. 'Huh?'

'Flick's coming, if she's not still grounded. You should come too. Right, Flick?' she said, turning her attention to me. 'Don't you think he should come?'

'Um –'

'It's OK,' Cal said quickly, reading my expression, 'thanks for the invite, though.'

'Well, feel free to come along if you change your mind.'

Sky waved and breezed back through the kitchen, thanking the team for having her before disappearing up the stairs.

I felt awkward as Cal began clearing up the pancake ingredients. I tried to think of something to say to break the uncomfortable atmosphere – something like how the party would be rubbish anyway and he wouldn't be missing out. But something stopped me as I formed the words in my brain and I felt ... guilty. Maybe because he'd been nice about my spectacular culinary skills.

'Hey,' I said quietly, picking up the butter, 'you should come.'

He lifted his eyes to meet mine but didn't say anything.

'I'm serious,' I insisted, sensing his confusion. 'You should come to the party.'

'Really?'

'Yeah.' I shrugged.

'Are you sure?'

'Yeah. It will be . . . fun. BUT,' I added sharply, making him jump, 'on the condition that you stop making that stupid joke about us dating.'

'Deal.'

He smiled at me and I smiled back.

'Right, then.' He rolled up his sleeves. 'You hungry?'

'Yes.'

'Good.' He grinned, taking the butter from me. 'Because I make a mean pancake.'

SIXTEEN

The forks came back to haunt me. But this time, a week since my kitchen experience, I was ready for them.

I was pretty confident that learning which fork went where on a place setting would be easier than having to pluck a pheasant, which by the way is DISGUSTING . . . and at the same time, very satisfying. Chef even said I was a natural at it, a comment I was sure to repeat to Mum that evening. She came in to find me lying on the sofa with my feet up and a cold compress on my head, and went, 'Ah, so you really did spend the day in the kitchen,' in this knowledgeable voice, like some kind of wise wizard.

After telling her that all the chefs deserved a raise and a medal for how much stress they experience every day, I informed her about Chef noting my innate talents at plucking poultry, thinking that she might reply like a normal parent and say something about how wonderful I am.

That did not happen.

Instead, she just raised her eyebrows and said, 'Well, you've always been good at tearing things apart,' and then went into her study, telling me not to disturb her as she was about to make an important conference call. I was too exhausted to tell her off for being so dismissive of her star child and ended up falling asleep on the sofa a few minutes later, giving Fritz the perfect opportunity to unwind the toilet roll all over the flat, undisturbed by either of us.

Matthew had taken some days off to spend time with Cal during half-term, so my next 'Royale education' day, – aka the Day of Forks – wasn't until the following Saturday, which left me with nothing to do all week, considering I wasn't allowed to leave the hotel, except to walk Fritz. Jamie, the sommelier/dog walker, accompanied me most days to the nearest park and I used the opportunities to ask him exactly what a sommelier does.

Turns out, it's quite a lot. I don't know how he finds time to walk Fritz.

He has daily meetings with Chef to learn about the menu and make sure the wine list will complement it, and he knows everything about every bottle of wine in the cellar. Nothing gets selected for the wine list without him going to the vineyard where it's made, meeting the owner and tasting the wine.

'Great perk of the job,' he told me, even though it sounded like a very long process just for one type of wine. 'I get to travel the world.' When I pressed him to say at least one bad thing about the job, he mentioned the exams were quite hard work. But even then, he kind of enjoyed them as he loved tasting the wine, thinking what food he would pair it with, and 'finding its notes'. I told him not to be so cringe about the whole thing but he just laughed at me.

When I wasn't throwing sticks for Fritz and learning about mouthfeel from Jamie, I spent most of my half-term annoying Audrey. She palmed me off to Matthew's second-in-command, Harry, for a couple of days, and it turns out that, when you put your mind to it, the booking system is the easiest thing in the world. Harry and I laughed about Matthew glorifying what is essentially a spreadsheet leading to another spreadsheet, and he even let me book in a couple of reservations, which he highlighted in yellow so that he could show Matthew the ones I had done when he returned.

'Why yellow?' I asked, as he picked the colour.

'Yellow suits you. It's the closest to gold.' He smiled charmingly.

Mum could really take a leaf from Harry's book.

I started to get into a little routine throughout the week

– first thing in the morning, I'd drop by the kitchen to grab breakfast, and say hello to Chef, Sasha and the team; I'd help Timothy make coffee for the early-rising guests and then would take a cup to Harry (flat white), Audrey (one-shot latte) and, if I could find her, Mum (double espresso). Then I would help Harry with bits and bobs at the front desk, aided greatly by Fritz, who was really starting to work his winter wardrobe.

Fritz's Instagram page had always had a good following but recently it had gone stratospheric since Sky mentioned it on her own feed. He now had more followers than any other pet on Instagram and he was getting sent more freebies than ever. Lewis Blume sent me and Fritz matching jumpers, which went down a storm, and I was starting to be a bit more creative with his headwear, although I could only put hats on him for the few seconds that it took for me to take the photo. He tried to eat the flat cap sent to him from Chanel.

But the best gift of all came from Prince Gustav Xavier III: a brand-new selfie stick, with tiny little bones and sausage-dog silhouettes engraved in gold all along in it.

Towards the end of the week, Audrey finally let me tag along with her, so I left Fritz front of house in Harry's capable hands, and joined her in her daily meetings with the heads of department. When we were in a meeting with Ellie, the head of events, Audrey was torn between two different ideas to present to a client for their party theme. She listened as Ellie took her through them both, and then swivelled in her chair to look at me.

'What do you think?'

'Me?'

'Yes.'

'I think the floral one.'

'Why?' Audrey asked.

'Um . . .'

'Just say what you think,' she encouraged.

'I think it suits the hostess of the party better. I met her when she came to the hotel the other day for her meeting with Ellie. We were chatting and I don't know –' I shrugged – 'I just think that floral theme suits her personality.'

Audrey and Ellie shared a glance, before a smile spread across Audrey's face.

'I completely agree. It does suit her. Thank you, Flick.'

I couldn't believe that Audrey had actually been interested in MY opinion. The only other time that had ever happened was a couple of years ago when she was going to the hairdresser's and I'd said she would look good with a fringe. She came in with one the next day.

I was very wrong about the fringe.

On Saturday morning, I found Mum in one of the

meeting rooms, checking that everything was in order for her first appointment. I put her double espresso on the table and went to leave.

'Flick,' she said, as I reached the door, 'I spoke to Audrey this morning. She told me you've been wonderful this week. Helping Harry and the staff. She also mentioned that you greatly helped her with a very important client event.'

'Not really –' I shrugged – 'Audrey just asked for my opinion, which was nice of her.'

'She told me what happened and I have to say, I'm extremely pleased. Making an event special and unique to the client is all about taking into account what they are like as a person. Your instincts were spot on.'

'Thanks.'

'Off you go, then,' she said, returning to her papers.

I scurried out and closed the door. For the first time in a *long* time, I felt that I had really made Mum proud of me. I couldn't work out if that was a good thing or not. I mean, it felt nice and everything but if I kept this whole making-parents-happy thing up I was in danger of turning into Cal Weston.

'I don't believe it.'

Timothy blinked and slowly lowered himself into a chair to let the shock sink in.

Cal chuckled. 'It's truly a miracle, isn't it?'

I sighed. 'Ye of little faith! I have mastered the forks.'

Timothy ran his finger across the line of forks, the perfectly folded napkin, the knives and the spoons. He shook his head.

'It's perfect. You did it!' Timothy exclaimed. 'You were actually *listening*.'

'It took me ages, though,' I admitted, looking down at my handiwork. 'You do it in a matter of seconds.'

'Ah,' he said, 'that's just practice.'

We were interrupted by a waitress, Poppy, who shyly asked Timothy for help with a difficult table upstairs. He excused himself and rushed out after her.

We were in Chef's office – it had taken me all morning to get the place settings just right, and we'd had to move downstairs from the restaurant because guests began arriving for the lunchtime service. I'd kept putting the forks in the wrong order, or mixing up the white wine glasses with the red or dessert wine glasses, and don't even get me started on how to fold a napkin. Who decided napkins should be so flimsy?

'Never again will I be intimidated by forks,' I

announced, sitting down.

Cal was sitting at Chef's desk, studying the new menu. 'The world can rejoice,' he commented, before a look of disappointment washed over his expression. 'The strawberry mousse is gone!'

'Yes, Chef felt that was a summer pudding. But don't worry, the plum and almond cake he's introduced to the menu is incredible,' I enthused. 'You'll love it.'

Watching him as he ran his eyes down the menu, I guess I could kind of see what Sky meant when we talked on Wednesday – I'd been sitting in her room while she got ready to go to the stadium for one of her tour concerts, and she'd turned the conversation to Cal.

'So, that guy in the kitchen –' she began, pulling her hoodie over her head. Her costumes, hair and make-up were all done at the venue so whenever she left for her concerts, it just looked as though she was leaving to go to the gym. 'He's cute.'

'Chef?' I wrinkled my nose, flicking through a magazine with Sky on its cover. 'Isn't he a bit old for you?'

'No, not Chef!' She laughed, picking up her trainers. 'That Cal guy. You've talked about him but you never mentioned that he was tall and handsome.'

I lowered the magazine to watch her doing up her laces. 'Really? You think he's hot?'

'He's got that cute vibe going for him. His dimples are adorable.'

'He's also SUCH a nerd,' I pointed out. 'He reads books about tanks and London architecture. In his free time.'

'Geek chic.' She shrugged.

'I've never really thought about him like that. He's always just been there, lurking around the hotel like a loner.'

'He seemed nice,' she said, attempting to tame her wild hair, clipping it back from her face. 'Anyway, whatever, let me tell you about my date to the Christmas Ball.'

'The dancer?'

'No, he fell through. But I've managed to bag myself a European prince.'

With Cal distracted by the menu, I took the opportunity to really look at him. I guess it was quite cute the way his thick hair was always sticking up at odd angles, and he did have nice green eyes. A gentle, olive green. And I suppose he did have those dimples, which some people might find attractive.

'OK, what is it?' He suddenly sighed, bringing his eyes up to meet mine.

'Nothing,' I said quickly, straightening up and knocking all my forks out of place.

'You're looking at me weirdly,' he pointed out. 'Do I have something on my face?'

'No, no, your face is good. I mean, it's fine. It's got nothing on it.' I moved the forks back into position, feeling flustered. 'I wasn't looking at you. I was looking . . . at something else. Anyway, how was your half-term?'

'It was good. I heard you were kept busy.'

'Yeah, I learned a lot. Hey, did you know that your dad once stepped in as a film producer's assistant? The producer was staying here and freaked out when his assistant quit on the first day of filming, so your dad offered his services and got Harry to cover him.'

Cal smiled. 'Yeah, that's a great story.'

'Typical of your dad, always going the extra mile.'

'Typical of the Royale, you mean.'

I looked at him quizzically.

'Everyone here goes above and beyond,' he explained, putting the menu down on the desk. 'They make sure that everything is perfect. Don't you think?'

'Yeah, I guess. How do you know so much about them? And the hotel?' I asked, leaning back in my chair.

'What do you mean?'

'You know everything and everyone in this place, and they all know you. How?'

He ran a hand through his hair and fidgeted with the corner of the menu.

'I don't know, I just hang out here a lot. And because of Dad.'

'It's more than that,' I insisted. 'That's why Audrey told me to ask you to help me learn about everything – she said that, apart from Mum and maybe her, you were the person who knew how the whole operation worked.'

He shrugged. 'I've done a bit of extra research recently.'

I opened my mouth to probe him further but Timothy popped his head round the door.

'How would you like to learn about serving a table?'

'Great idea.' Cal jumped to his feet, looking relieved at the interruption.

I rolled my eyes. Only Cal Weston would think learning how to serve a table was a *great* idea.

We lined up with the other waiters and took the plates that Chef passed to us, after he had scrutinised each one. Timothy explained how each seat around a table was numbered in the heads of the waiters, so they could remember which dish went to which diner without having to ask them what they'd ordered. My dish was for guest number three.

I followed the other waiters into the centre table of the dining room, carrying a goat's cheese and walnut starter.

Then I saw who guest number three at the table was.

Ella.

She was looking decidedly bored, with her mum and three other ladies, who must have been her mum's friends. Our eyes met and after looking momentarily surprised, a thin, satisfied smile crept across her face.

I hadn't heard from Ella once throughout half-term. Grace had messaged almost every day but I hadn't heard one peep from Ella, and I hadn't really considered texting her. Seeing her now, it dawned on me that I hadn't missed her at all.

'Flick,' she said curiously, as I placed her starter in front of her, 'what are you doing?'

'Serving,' I replied politely. 'How has your half-term been?'

'*Serving?*' She sniggered, ignoring my question. Then she saw Cal putting a plate down on the opposite side of the table. 'Hang on a second, is this what Cal meant when he said you were going on a date? Oh my God, wait until everyone hears about this! How *embarrassing!*'

She cackled loudly. Anger bubbled up through me as Cal's face flushed beetroot-red, Ella's mum and friends stared and all the other waiters stood awkwardly, not knowing what to do.

'Actually, Ella,' I announced, holding up my chin, 'if

I'm going to run this place one day, I need to know exactly how it works, from top to bottom. Isn't that right, Cal?'

He hesitated. Catching his eye, I smiled encouragingly.

'Yeah,' he replied, 'that's right.'

'Enjoy your starters, ladies,' I continued, as Ella continued to sneer, 'and let us know if there's anything else we can get you. Welcome to Hotel Royale.'

And with that, I walked out confidently, under the intrigued gaze of everyone in the room. My mum was standing next to Audrey at the door, with a stunned expression on her face. And I could have sworn her eyes were twinkling as she watched me leave.

Hey, you going to Sky's party next week?

Hey Ethan, I hope so! How have you been?

Great. We can talk details about your guest vlog. See you then

SEVENTEEN

Ella wasn't speaking to me. Which made hanging out with my friends back at school really quite difficult. In fact, it was impossible. Any time I got near Grace, Ella would whisk her away from me as though I was spreading vicious germs, and whenever I walked past, Ella and her new minions would whisper something and then all turn to stare. On Monday, I just shrugged it off, telling myself it would be sorted by the next day, but it just got worse. By Friday, I resigned myself to the fact that whatever this was, it wasn't going to blow over.

The whole thing was so stupid; if anyone should have been mad, it should have been me. Ella was the one who made the horrible comment; *I* was nothing but nice to her. Instead, there was a rumour going round that I'd lied about hanging out with celebrities – in fact I'd just been waiting on them.

Ella was meant to be my friend but she sure wasn't acting like it. She seemed to be enjoying spreading rumours about me. I felt sad about Grace too. I missed our weird conversations, and I could tell she felt awkward about everything. She kept throwing me longing looks down the hallways and across classrooms, but couldn't seem to find the courage to face Ella's wrath and come to talk to me. It wouldn't have been so bad if I had loads of other friends, but weirdly, even though I'd always known that I was the most popular girl in my class, I had no idea who to actually hang out with now. I had always been part of Ella's pack – or rather, *she'd* been part of mine – and now I had gone solo, I came to the quick realisation that I didn't know anyone outside that group, not properly.

I felt safe in the knowledge that as soon as I appeared on Ethan's vlog or was photographed at Sky's party, my friends would come flocking back and Ella would be stuck on her own. That didn't make lunchtimes any easier in the meantime, though. I had no idea where to sit, so on Monday I just sat on my own, at the end of a table of boys from two years above, who barely noticed me because they were so engrossed in talking about computer games.

After another solitary lunch on Tuesday, I dreaded a repeat on Wednesday, so I bought some crisps and a chocolate bar from the vending machine and hid in the corner of the library. Mr Grindle was in the staffroom having his lunch so I could eat in peace – that is, until I was disturbed by Cal. The last person I wanted to meet.

He looked totally stunned to see me. 'What are you doing in here?'

'Reading.'

'You don't have a book.'

Damn his stupid logic.

'I'm about to read. I was just having a sit-down first. Is that a crime?'

'What are you really doing in here, Flick?'

I let out a long drawn-out sigh and then told him the truth about having no one to sit with at lunch. I thought he'd feel all sorry for me but instead he just laughed, which was incredibly rude and inappropriate. So I told him so.

'That is incredibly rude and inappropriate.'

'I'm sorry.' He chuckled, not looking sorry at all. 'But it's just that, well, now you know how it feels.'

'How what feels?' I said angrily. 'Being a loser?'

He shrugged. 'Yeah.'

'Huh?'

'Come on, Flick,' he continued, 'this is how the other half lives. While you and Ella enjoy looking down your noses at everyone and acting as though you're in some kind of elite club, this is how everyone outside it feels.

Anyway,' he added chirpily, 'I've got to return these books. Enjoy your lunch!'

And then he had the cheek to just walk off and leave me there.

Even though he had acted outrageously and I considered never talking to him again, I slowly accepted that Cal may have had a point. The next day at school, I noticed that people tended to keep their heads down and speed up in the corridor as they passed wherever Ella and her gang were standing. Every now and then, Ella would see someone approaching and whisper something to the gang, who would turn right on cue to watch that singled-out person pass. And that person would always look nervous and go bright red. The only person who didn't have that reaction was Cal. He passed them without taking any notice and, due to recent events, there was more whispering and pointing at him than ever.

Not as much as I got, though.

On Friday, I sat at my now-usual table in the library with a delicious pasta dish Chef had made me. I'd told him what was going on at school and he'd gone all red in the face and then exploded.

'Well!' he yelled after he had finished ranting about Ella. 'I certainly won't be letting you go hungry. If they

231

won't let you eat in the cafeteria, then you will dine like a queen in the library.'

And then he'd created the poshest lunchbox of all time, complete with a starter, main and pudding. It almost made not having any friends a good thing.

Cal had returned that book on London architecture to the library, so I had sneaked it from the shelf and started reading the chapter on the Royale. It turns out there were loads of cool facts in there, like how, when it was being built in the 1900s, one of the builders, a Mr Colin Whittle, was convinced that he kept seeing a ghost appearing from its walls. He quit his job and tried to garner support from the other workers to have the building work halted but no one believed him. He ended up begging to come back but they didn't let him.

I couldn't help but feel that Mr Colin Whittle and I had a lot in common, now that I too had been shunned from society. Except, you know, my situation was maybe a little less paranormal.

I was just reading the Colin Whittle story and freaking out about that time my earrings vanished into thin air – and how they may not have been eaten by Fritz as I'd thought but stolen by this ghost – when I heard footsteps come up and stop next to me. I rolled my eyes and turned to tell Cal to leave me alone, when I found myself staring up at Olly.

'Hey.' He pulled out the chair next to me and sat in it.

I glanced around, checking to see if this was some kind of cruel joke where Ella jumped out at me and poured a bucket of custard over my head or something, but I couldn't see anyone else through the stacks of books.

'It's OK,' he said, reading my panicked expression. 'It's just me.' He gestured at my pasta. 'That looks amazing.'

'It is.'

'I'm really sorry about the way Ella's treating you,' he said.

'Oh.' I relaxed, comforted that this definitely wasn't a joke and he was here of his own accord. He was doing that being-nice thing again. 'Don't worry, it's nothing to do with you.'

'It's not cool,' he noted. 'I don't even really understand what you did wrong.'

'That makes two of us.' I smiled, twirling pasta on my fork.

'She just likes the power of putting people down,' he said bitterly. 'I broke up with her.'

I stopped twisting my fork. 'What?'

'I mean, we weren't even really going out.' He sighed,

leaning back in his chair and running his fingers through his hair. 'I don't even like her.'

He caught my eye and I couldn't help but burst out laughing. He looked surprised at first but then he started laughing too.

'Stupid, right?'

'So stupid.' I giggled. 'Why were you dating someone you didn't like?'

'I don't know!'

We exploded into a fresh round of laughter and then he leaned forwards and put a hand on my wrist. I had to admit that Ella was right about one thing: Olly's eyelashes were insanely long, especially close up. And they were so neat. Framing those deep, dark eyes so perfectly. Have they always been that neat? I don't remember his lashes being so neat.

The word 'neat' began to lose all meaning in my head.

'On Monday, don't hide in the library. Come to lunch. Sit with me.'

'NEAT.'

OH MY GOD, WHY DOES THIS KEEP HAPPENING?

'Neat?' He laughed. 'I've never heard you use that expression before.'

'Uh,' I began, 'I'm thinking of bringing it back. Neat. It's a good word. Don't you think? We should use it more. Neat.'

I hate my brain.

'If you say so.'

As he stood up to leave, our gaze broke and I was able to pull my brain into gear.

'Olly,' I said quickly, 'she won't like it. I mean, you need to really think about it, if you sit with me at lunch. She'll be cross with you and probably won't talk to you again. Trust me, I know what she's like. I completely understand if you don't want to risk that.'

He sighed.

'Flick, I no longer have any hairs on my arm due to her constant possessive stroking. Her not talking to me would be a good thing.'

And he walked away, leaving me to my pasta. I just wasn't feeling so hungry any more.

He must have told Grace about it because that evening I was giving Fritz his weekly bubble bath, when the landline rang. It was Matthew, telling me that Grace was in reception, asking for me. I told him she could come up and as I wrapped Fritz in his favourite fluffy towel, I hugged him close, suddenly feeling sick with nerves. I opened the door when the bell rang to see Grace sheepishly holding several packs of microwave popcorn and two tubs of ice cream.

'Movie night? Since you missed last weekend's.'

I didn't know what to say, so I just stood aside to let her come in. She went to perch on the sofa. I followed her and sat opposite, placing Fritz, who was now fast asleep in his little towel, next to me, and waiting for her to speak.

'I'm so sorry about school,' she wailed. 'I've hated everything this week and I just really want us to be friends again!'

I passed her a tissue. 'We are friends, Grace.'

'Ella's been so mean and I told her not to say horrible things about you and then she snapped at me and said that you had never liked me in the first place and had always said nasty things about me behind my back, so I didn't know what to do. And then Olly broke up with her and now she hates me even more, and then Olly said I'd been a really bad friend to you, and . . .' Her lip quivered. 'Everything is awful!'

I held out another tissue and waited patiently while she mopped herself up and blew her nose, which woke Fritz up. He growled and then buried himself back into the towel.

'It's OK,' I said, coming to sit next to her and giving her a comforting pat on the knee.

'It's not OK,' she whined.

'Yeah, it is. You haven't been a bad friend. I know what Ella can be like.'

'So, we're still friends?' She sniffed, her big eyes blinking hopefully through her tears.

'Yeah, we're still friends.' I smiled.

'Phew!' She launched herself at me for a hug. 'I'm so pleased,' she said with a watery smile, pulling away and shuffling comfortably into the back of the sofa. 'And you know what? I don't think I'll miss being friends with Ella. I've been on constant eggshells this whole term. It's exhausting.'

I laughed. 'You can relax now. We'll face her together.'

She pulled off the lid of one of the tubs of ice cream. 'So. Movie night?'

'Sounds perfect.'

Mum said Grace could stay over, so she set her up a mattress on the floor and we talked for hours, which Fritz got very grumpy about. He kept gnawing loudly at the edge of his bed in an attempt to communicate to us to shut up and stop disturbing his beauty sleep, but it was the first time I'd actually properly talked to Grace without her being afraid of saying something wrong, so I found out loads about her that I had no idea about. Like how she loves animals – especially dogs and tortoises – so she wants to be a vet when she's older, and she's also this massive film buff with a thing for old movies that no one has ever heard of. According to Grace, they don't make them like they used to. In a few hours of chatting, I learned more about Grace than after weeks of hanging out.

I didn't mind that we didn't stop talking until the early hours of the next morning. I drifted off to sleep happy in the knowledge that I had absolutely nothing to do the next day.

I couldn't have been more wrong.

EIGHTEEN

Someone was shaking me awake. I pulled up my eye mask to find Audrey staring down at me.

'What are you doing here?' I croaked, sitting up and rubbing my eyes. The mattress on the floor was empty. 'Where's Grace?'

'She's making coffee,' Audrey said, her brow furrowed. 'She let me into the flat. She's already showered and dressed and your mum has left for the lecture she's giving in Surrey.'

'Urgh, I should have known Grace is a morning person. She's so . . . chirpy.'

'You need to get up,' Audrey instructed, standing and throwing my towel at me.

'No, I don't,' I grumbled. 'I haven't arranged to shadow anyone today. Why doesn't anyone sleep in this place? You're all robots.'

'It's not that, it's Miss Chase.'

'Sky?' I rubbed my eyes. 'What do you mean?'

'Look at your phone. She's been trying to contact you

all morning. She rang reception in a state and asked if you could go and see her straight away.' Audrey bit her lip. 'She sounded strained on the phone. I think something's wrong.'

I reached for my phone and found missed calls, several 'SOS' texts and instructions to get my 'butt' in her room as soon as I could. I flung my duvet off and raced into the shower, coming out to find Audrey gone and Grace sitting on my bed, with the bed sheets stripped from her mattress and folded neatly in a pile. She looked so fresh and pretty, with her big bright eyes and clear skin, and her long black hair tied back neatly in a ponytail. In comparison, I'd caught a glimpse of myself in the bathroom mirror and actually yelped out loud in horror.

'Morning!' she greeted me cheerfully, holding out a mug of coffee, which I took gratefully. 'I added a bit of vanilla, I hope you like it.'

'Uh, thanks.' I took a sip after pulling on jeans and a jumper. 'Wow, that's amazing.'

'Audrey said you had to rush off. She explained that Skylar Chase needs your help. That is SO cool.'

'I'm sorry, Grace, I know I said we'd hang out.'

'Can I walk Fritz?'

I sat in front of the dressing table and brushed my wet hair. 'What? Now?'

'Yeah!' She smiled. 'I took him out while you were sleeping this morning but I think he needs a longer walk.'

'What time did you get up?' I asked, attempting to find a matching pair of shoes from the pile in the corner of my room.

'Early.' She shrugged. 'So can I? Walk him, I mean. It might be useful if you don't have to worry about him today. I can look after him.'

'Knock yourself out.'

She happily stood up and went to fetch his lead and collar from the kitchen, before popping her head round the door to say goodbye and to throw me one of my shoes she'd found in the sitting room.

'Aha! Thank you,' I said, shoving it on. 'See you later.'

'See you. Oh –' she held up her phone – 'and Olly says hey.'

☽ ♡ ✦

I had barely knocked on Sky's door when it swung open and she went, 'Where have you BEEN?'

I followed her into the suite where she flopped on to one of the sofas. Her entourage were dotted around the room, yelling into their phones. I picked my way through them to get to Sky, trying not to get in their way as they paced back and forth.

She looked terrible. For her. Which actually means she still looked better than most of the world's population but not so good by her usual standards. Her eyes were red and squinty, like she'd been crying, and she was wearing a jumper several sizes too big for her and some kind of bizarre Aladdin-style trousers.

'What's happened?' I asked, coming to sit down next to her as a message beeped through on her phone. She read it and then cried out, throwing her phone across the room, narrowly missing several members of her team – not that they cared, they were too busy shouting into their own phones to notice one go flying past their heads. I hadn't actually seen her entourage in its full force before. There were DOZENS of them, making the massive suite seem tiny, and they were all talking so loudly, it seemed impossible that they were able to hear whoever they were speaking to on the phone, but somehow they managed to continue their conversations. One of them was dodging through the crowd passing everyone cups of black coffee. I dreaded to think what the blood pressure average was in this room.

'Whoa, OK, diva pop star alert!' I exclaimed, having watched Sky's phone land. 'What's going on?'

'It's my party.' She sobbed. 'It's ruined. Completely ruined.'

'Why?'

'The club where it was going to be held has been shut down. This morning. What are the chances?'

'But the party is –'

'TONIGHT!' She crumpled into tears.

'Surely you can find a new venue. You're Skylar Chase!'

'You'd think,' she wailed, 'but everywhere good is booked. We can't just hold it at any old place, and we need to let all the guests know ... Argh, the press will have a field day! And I fly back to LA tomorrow, so I can't have it another evening. This is a disaster.'

I watched her as she buried her head in her hands. For some reason, as I watched her acting so distressed, something Cal had said popped into my head. Hotel Royale always goes the extra mile. Here was our most important guest and she was having a meltdown that was going to ruin all her memories of being in London. I had to do something.

'It's not a disaster,' I whispered. 'I know what to do.'

She blinked up at me. 'Huh?'

I stood up on the sofa and at the top my lungs, I yelled, 'EVERYONE, STOP TALKING!'

They all whipped their heads round to look at me and,

after glancing at Sky who gave them a firm nod, they told whoever they were speaking to they would call them back and lowered their phones.

'Right,' I said confidently, now that I had their attention, 'you can stop panicking. The party will be here. At Hotel Royale.'

Sky gasped. 'But . . . are there any rooms? At this late notice? On a Saturday?'

'You don't need to worry about anything. That's my job. Here's the plan of action,' I instructed, feeling all important standing up there on the sofa looking down at everyone. No wonder world leaders always speak from podiums. 'Sky, you are to relax today and get ready for your party this evening. I need someone to make sure that happens. Who can do that?'

Her assistant's hand shot up.

'Excellent. Thank you. Now, I just need to make a quick phone call.'

I jumped down from the sofa, grabbed the phone and dialled Audrey's office. She picked up straight away and gave me the information I asked for. I hung up and turned back to my silent audience, who were all watching in tense anticipation.

'I need all of you to go to the conference room on the second floor. Someone will be here in a minute to show you the way. The most important thing is that everyone calms down.' I gave them my biggest smile. 'We've got this.'

And then, with a salute at Sky, who was looking completely baffled, I left the room and raced down to Audrey. As per my phone instructions, she was waiting for me in her office with Matthew, Chef and Ellie. Cal waved at me from where he was comfortably sitting in Audrey's chair.

'Why aren't you sleeping like a normal teenager?' I asked him. 'Am I the only person in the world who has heard of lie-ins?'

'Next door neighbours arguing,' he explained, 'woke us up at 4 a.m. I was bored at home.'

'Flick, what's going on?' Audrey's expression was full of concern.

I launched into an explanation of what had happened to Sky. 'So, I've told her we'll have the party here,' I concluded.

'What do you mean?' Audrey asked.

'Here. At Hotel Royale.'

They stared in silence.

'But,' Audrey continued, 'how on earth can we do that, at such late notice? It's impossible.'

'Not at the Royale,' I corrected her. 'Nothing is impossible here. Right, Matthew?'

Matthew puffed his chest out like a peacock. 'That's right.'

'But we don't have any rooms available,' Ellie said, scrolling through her iPad to check.

'Nothing?' I asked, biting my lip. 'What about the conference rooms?'

'That won't work. They're too near the bedrooms, we'd disturb our guests.'

'There's got to be somewhere,' I insisted desperately. I couldn't let Sky down. She was counting on me. And no one ever counts on me.

She shook her head. 'We don't have any space available.'

I leaned back on Audrey's desk, totally deflated.

'Yes, we do,' Cal said softly.

We all turned to look at him. His eyes locked with mine.

'We have a space,' he insisted. 'It's available, it's out of the way, it's a bit kooky. It's even got its own mini terrace. It just needs a bit of . . . tidying.'

I was about to tell him off for using the word 'kooky' but then it suddenly clicked in my head what he was talking about.

'But Cal, we can't, it's your hideaway. It wouldn't be secret any more.'

'This is more important.' He nodded firmly. 'Flick, it's *perfect*.'

'I guess if we cleared it out, it would be big enough,' I said, considering.

'It's near the kitchens, easy to carry food and drink to and from.'

'A band or DJ could fit into the far corner, and there would be enough dance space.'

'We could put fairy lights down the tunnels, it would look amazing.'

'Or we can tell the guests to come to the outside door via the back road and through into the room that way.'

'Yes, you're a genius! We could line the road with lanterns leading them to it.'

'Magical and mysterious! It's perfect!'

'ENOUGH!' Matthew stepped forwards. 'What on EARTH are you two talking about?'

Cal and I grinned at each other like a couple of Cheshire cats.

'Come on.' I smiled. 'We'll show you.'

NINETEEN

> ### THE DAILY POST
>
> # The Party's Over for Skylar Chase!
>
> By Nancy Rose
>
> There's trouble in paradise. The Daily Post has just learned that the famous London nightclub, Candle Bar, is temporarily shutting its doors due to emergency building repairs, leaving Skylar Chase in the lurch for her all-important star-studded London party that was scheduled to take place there tonight! According to a close source, the American pop star, due back in LA tomorrow, is devastated. 'She's in bits,' the source disclosed. 'This meant a lot to her and now she'll likely have to cancel the event.' We have contacted Miss Chase's representative but so far they have declined to comment. Sorry, Skylar, but looks like your party's over! You can cry if you want to . . .

'The party is not over,' I announced to the conference room, where Sky's entourage had gathered. 'I can confirm that we can hold it here tonight.'

They burst into applause and whoops, immediately getting their phones out at the ready.

'But –' I held up my hands to quieten them – 'it's going to be a lot of work and we'll need all hands on deck. Let's just say that the room we've got available isn't exactly your average party venue.' I shared a smile with Cal. 'Let me introduce you to the team.'

I gestured to Audrey, Matthew, Cal, Chef and Ellie, who were all standing in a line next to me. They waved to the crowd.

'We need a group of volunteers to help Cal clean out the venue and set it up. Chef and Sasha are going to be sorting canapés and Jamie will be in charge of drinks, so I'm going to need someone from Sky's team to select from a list of food options. Audrey has called in our florist, who will be arriving any minute. They will be in charge of decorations. We need someone from your team to get in touch with Sky's record company and get promotional material, anything they want on display when it comes to the latest album. Ellie is going to be sorting out the sound system, lights and any electrical equipment that we'll need – can someone liaise with her about a DJ? She's also going to book an official photographer. We have one on speed dial. Matthew will be in charge of the guest list;

we need a confirmed one in the next half an hour so we can be sure of capacity and how much food we need to provide. We also need to make sure that each guest confirms they're aware of the change of location. And –' I took a deep breath – 'I will be overseeing everything. If you have any questions or problems, you come to me. OK, now work out who of your team is doing what.'

They huddled together excitedly. I noticed Audrey watching me with a funny look on her face.

'What?'

She hesitated. 'It's just, you really reminded me of your mother just then.'

'What, bossing everyone around?'

'No.' She smiled. 'Taking charge.'

I don't know how we managed it, but it worked.

As soon as Sky's entourage had delegated people to each task, everyone leaped into action and by the evening, what used to be mine and Cal's bizarre secret storeroom and escape exit, now looked like the most exclusive party venue in the city. It had been completely cleared and, thanks to Amy and her team, it was sparkling clean. A huge canvas of Sky's latest album cover was hanging on the wall, lit up by white globe lamps and masses of fairy lights, twinkling everywhere. The florist had created an archway of flowers over the door frames and all over the tiny patio, so walking through into the room, it was as though you were entering a scene from *Alice's Adventures in Wonderland*. Jamie had even created bespoke drinks for the evening, which Timothy and his colleagues were ready to serve, and the canapés looked too perfect – Chef informed me that Sasha had insisted on taking charge of them. He was so impressed with her, he told me proudly, that she was now in line for a promotion.

With guests due to arrive any minute – guided by lanterns set up all down the back road – Cal and I nervously led Sky down through the tunnels to see what she thought. Dressed in a sparkling silver Lewis Blume dress and bright royal blue heels, she tottered down the now-lit maze of corridors and into her party. Her eyes filled with tears as she stepped into the room and took it all in.

'It's . . . beautiful.'

She reached for my hand and squeezed it.

'It's perfect,' she whispered. 'I can't believe you did all of this.'

'All in a day's work.' I laughed.

She pulled us both in for a giant hug and, while her

assistant diverted her attention to check the guest list, Cal and I hurried off to get ready.

Grace was on the sofa, eating popcorn and discussing the works of Tim Burton with Fritz, while *Edward Scissorhands* played in the background. I had run up earlier to fill her in on everything that was going on and – after she'd had to go splash her face with cold water because of the shock – she had been super helpful, promising me she would look after Fritz for the day. And there she was waiting, just like she'd said. Not only that, but she'd gone through my wardrobe and put out a variety of 'pop-star-party-appropriate' outfits on my bed for me to choose from. We went with skinny black jeans and a red off-the-shoulder top, with my hair tied back in a high ponytail and striking red lipstick.

'Are you *sure* you can't come?' I asked Grace, examining myself in the mirror.

'I WISH, but it's my granny's birthday party.' She sighed, looking very pained. 'Mum would KILL me if I missed it. Even for Skylar Chase and a celebrity party.'

'I've been there before.' I nodded. 'I promise I'll try to introduce you to her at some point soon, OK? I mean it. Maybe when she's back for the Christmas Ball.'

'Thanks! You look amazing, by the way. Not as good as Fritz, though,' she added, doing up the last few buttons of his tuxedo and straightening his bow tie.

'Fritz, you're so handsome!' I scooped him up under my arm.

'You both look great and tonight is going to be such a big success,' she enthused, pulling on her jacket and picking up all her things. 'You've got nothing to worry about.'

'Thanks for being here today and looking after Fritz.'

'It was nice to chill out with him.' She gave him a pat on his head. 'Well, I'd better get going. Don't forget to call me tomorrow and tell me everything.'

'Grace.' I hesitated. 'I know that hanging out with me won't do much for your street cred –'

'Are you kidding? Flick –' she took my hands – 'you're about to host a party for Skylar Chase. You're the coolest person on the planet right now.'

'At school, I mean. And I just wanted to say that I really appreciate it. You coming over and everything.'

She smiled. 'Good luck with tonight.'

She scurried out and shut the door behind her, leaving Fritz and me alone.

In the silence, the pressure of tonight hit me like a ton of bricks. I'd been rushing about so much during the day, I hadn't even had time to really think about it. But here I was, standing in the hallway with the best-dressed sausage dog in London, about to go to a party I had organised for the biggest pop star in the world.

What happened if it went wrong? What happened if the lights all fell down or the music didn't work or there wasn't enough food? I mean, I'd told Chef to prepare double the amount just in case so surely that wouldn't happen. But what happened if no one even showed up? If something went wrong, it would all be my fault. My mouth was suddenly very dry. I was frozen to the spot. I couldn't go. I couldn't believe I'd put myself in this position. What had I been *thinking*?

I jumped as my phone buzzed loudly on the hallway table.

> Hey, Grace tells me you're a celeb party planner these days. Pretty awesome. Go smash it. Olly x

I read it, took a deep breath and turned to Fritz.

'You ready?'

He barked.

'Me too,' I announced, reaching for the door handle. It was time to go.

TWENTY

Cal hated me.

I stood waiting in reception the day after the party, hoping he might show up. I knew that I had ruined everything, and if it were the other way round, I wouldn't bother showing up either. Not after what I'd said.

But I still hoped that he might.

'It's not that bad,' Sky assured me, when I filled her in properly on Sunday morning. She was tired from the night before but the party had gone so well that nothing could dampen her spirits, not even the long-haul flight ahead of her. It couldn't have been more of a hit. Everyone on the guest list had shown up, from glamorous models to dramatic rock stars to showbiz journalists, and every celebrity website in the world was talking about it – the stars, the clothes, the venue. Ellie had been inundated with requests to hire out that room for the oncoming year of parties.

'We're going to need to hire more staff,' I overheard her telling Timothy during the party when she confirmed yet another booking.

I should have woken up the next morning elated by the evening's events. Instead, I woke up feeling like the worst person in the world. Not even Fritz howling along pitch-perfectly to David Bowie in the kitchen where Mum was making breakfast could make me feel better. I checked my phone: no messages.

'Why are you so upset anyway?' Sky asked, as her team busied themselves around her suite, packing up everything. Her flight back to LA was that afternoon, which only made me feel worse. Though at least she'd be flying back next month for the Christmas Ball.

I shrugged. 'I just feel . . . guilty.'

'But what you said was true, wasn't it?' She dodged out of the way of her assistant who came flying past clutching a handful of hair products.

'I guess. I just have this horrible feeling in my stomach. Like lead.'

She sighed and slumped down on to the sofa next to me.

'Tell me again exactly what happened.'

I had arrived downstairs at the party to find it brimming with famous faces greeting each other enthusiastically and posing together for photos. I made my way through the air-kissing crowd to get to Sky, who was talking to a journalist about her new album.

'– and learning from that relationship inspired several of the songs.' Her face lit up when she saw me hovering nearby with Fritz, and she gestured for me to join her.

'And have you enjoyed your trip to London?' the journalist asked, her Dictaphone light blinking red under Sky's nose.

'It's been the best, mostly because of new friends,' she replied, hauling me under her arm and giving Fritz a pat on the head. 'It's surprising how few of them you can find in showbiz.'

The journalist attempted to pry more information out of her but Sky had spotted Ethan waiting in the queue to get in, so she expertly moved her along by introducing her to her producer. Ethan kissed Sky's cheeks and admired the surroundings.

'Can't believe you pulled this off. I thought you were in big trouble this morning.'

'So did I –' Sky nodded – 'until Flick came along. This is all down to her.'

'Great,' he said, leaning forwards to kiss me on the cheek. He smelled so good, it made my knees go weak.

What IS his aftershave? I need to buy some to spray on my pillow or something.

Not in a creepy way.

'Ah, there's Jacob and Carly. Flick, I'll find you in a second.'

He disappeared into the crowd and I tried to ignore the sinking feeling of being brushed aside. I guess I couldn't expect him to only pay attention to me. He was definitely a master of playing it cool, whereas I turned into a lump of jelly whenever he came near. I needed to take a leaf out of Sky's book – her date to the Christmas Ball wasn't invited to this party as, according to her, that would make her look 'way too keen'.

Watching Ethan disappear into the crowd, I spotted Cal nudging his way through to me. I couldn't help but smile as he approached – for someone who never made an effort for anything except homework, he'd done a pretty good job of scrubbing up. He was wearing a crisp white shirt and a thin black tie, and had done something with his hair so it wasn't so fluffy.

'It's packed,' he enthused, passing me a drink. 'Everyone looks like they're having a good time. Cheers.'

We clinked our pink lemonade as Fritz, tucked under my arm, tried and failed to snaffle a canapé from a passing tray. I plonked him on the ground and it wasn't long before he was swept up into Jamie's arms and offered a crab cake.

'Couldn't have done this without you,' I admitted to Cal, as he laughed at Fritz being so spoiled.

He shook his head. 'Yeah, you could have. With your eyes closed. You've always been good at telling people what to do.'

I laughed.

'Nice lipstick, by the way,' he said, taking a sip of his drink. 'Looks good.'

I gave him a funny look.

'What?' he asked innocently.

'Nothing. It's just . . . you're being nice.'

'I'm always nice.'

'I know . . . well, I mean, you don't like me.'

'That's not true.'

Someone knocked me as they squeezed past, almost tipping my lemonade all over me. I looked down to check my dress for any stray spillages when I felt Cal's warm fingers grip my wrist. Our eyes locked.

'That's not true,' he repeated, in a lower, more serious voice. I was so surprised at the intense way he was looking at me, that I suddenly felt all the breath knocked out of me and a warm, giddy feeling in my stomach.

I really needed to stop being affected so much

by boys. How does anyone get anything done when they're walking around with their sincere eyes and shapely jaws?

Oh my God, I just used the word 'shapely'.

WHAT WAS WRONG WITH MY BRAIN?

'Flick?'

Cal dropped my wrist at my mum's voice.

'Mum! What are you doing here?'

'Well, my lecture's finished, and I came home to hear that I was hosting a party for Skylar Chase.'

I felt the colour drain out my face. I hadn't told Mum about the party earlier because I didn't want her to worry about anything. But I had meant to phone her beforehand to mention that the whole thing was happening, you know, it being her hotel and everything. But my panic after Grace leaving and then that really nice message from Olly had totally thrown my brain and I'd completely forgotten to call her.

'Mum, I meant to –'

'What a resounding success.' She beamed. 'Flick, I could not be more proud of you.'

She reached forwards and pulled me into a hug.

'Audrey told me everything,' she continued, releasing me to address Cal too. 'She said how you two clubbed together to arrange all of this and how hard you have both worked. I must say, I didn't realise this room even existed. How did you come across it?'

'Uh –'

'Well –'

'Um –'

'No matter.' She laughed, as Cal and I awkwardly mumbled, before putting on her sophisticated hotel-owner voice. 'Guests can always rely on Hotel Royale.'

'Right,' I agreed. 'That was the tagline we were channelling.'

'I'd better go and talk to Miss Chase,' she said, before placing a hand on my shoulder. 'Flick, I think it might be about time we talk about the Christmas Ball. Don't you?'

She smiled warmly at us and then strode away towards Sky. Without thinking, I threw my arms around Cal's neck, bouncing up and down on the spot.

'We did it! We did it!'

He laughed and suddenly I realised I was majorly invading Cal Weston's personal space, so I stumbled backwards, knocking into a grumpy supermodel behind me. After apologising to her, I turned back to Cal.

'Looks like you got your way.' He grinned.

'Duh!' I said, flicking my hair dramatically. 'As usual. Cal, thank you so –'

'Hey.' Ethan came out of nowhere, taking my hand

and shooting Cal an odd look. 'Can I steal you away? I need you to meet some people.'

'Right, yeah, of course.'

As he pulled me away from Cal, he smiled down at me curiously.

'Who is that guy? Do I need to be worried about riding solo to the Christmas Ball?'

'No, no!' I assured him quickly. 'He's nobody. Just the son of an employee.'

But Ethan wasn't listening any more. He had seen someone he knew and was too busy greeting them. I glanced back over my shoulder to see Cal watching me with a stunned, hurt look on his face. He shook his head, and then turned to push his way through the crowd and out the door. He didn't come back.

'He'll show,' Sky said determinedly as the last of her suitcases were taken downstairs by the porters. When I'd finished repeating the story to her, I'd mentioned that Cal and I had previously arranged a 'Royale education' lesson that Sunday with the florist.

I nodded with much more confidence than I felt and escorted her downstairs to where her car was waiting.

Mum, Audrey, Matthew and Fritz had lined up ready to say their goodbyes in the lobby.

'I'll miss you guys,' she said, her eyes welling as she picked Fritz up and he gave her a lick on the cheek. 'See you at Christmas.'

She gave me a long hug, took one last selfie with Fritz, blew us all kisses and then waltzed out the door through the crowd of waiting press and into her car. That was when the florist arrived ready for our day and the wait for Cal started.

He didn't show up.

TWENTY-ONE

'But the deal's off.' Cal shrugged simply.

I had accosted him in the cafeteria, the first time I'd seen him at school that day. He hadn't replied to any of my voicemails or texts, and I'd tried searching for him in the library earlier in the morning with no luck. But then as I was sliding a plate of food on to my tray at lunch, I spotted him putting his tray into the racks at the other side of the dining room, about to leave. I left my tray where it was, and raced through the cafeteria to catch him, dodging through students and causing heads to pop up curiously at the fuss. Ella, sitting in the middle of a table of girls, looked particularly interested.

'What do you mean the deal's off?' I asked, when I'd demanded that he explain why he hadn't shown up the day before. It's not like I hadn't apologised in those messages and, yes, what I said wasn't the kindest of comments but I explained in my voicemails that I hadn't meant it, so there was no need for him to be in such a strop.

He sighed as though having to explain something very simple to an impatient child.

'The deal between me and you.'

'I don't understand,' I said, crossing my arms. 'You said you would help me learn everything there was to know. There's still plenty to learn.'

'Yeah, and you said that in return you'd get me an interview with Skylar Chase and unless the *Daily Post* is completely mistaken, Skylar Chase took a plane back to LA yesterday.'

My heart sank. He was right. I had completely forgotten about his interview.

'Cal –'

He cut me off coldly. 'I held up my end of the deal and, as we found out on Saturday, you got your way. You can go to the Christmas Ball with your blogger or vlogger . . . or whatever he is. You didn't hold up your end of the deal, so as far as I'm concerned, it's all off. Surely you don't need the help of a mere son of an employee any more. After all, that's all I am, right? A nobody.'

'No, Cal, I didn't mean it. Didn't you get my messages?'

'I'll see you around, Flick.'

I wanted to go after him as he walked away, but I didn't know what else there was to say. I had become so involved in winning over Mum about the Christmas Ball,

I'd completely forgotten the promise I'd made to Cal. And he'd wasted all that time helping me to get what I wanted, without getting anything in return.

'Well, well, well.'

A snide voice behind me made a shiver go down my spine. I turned to face Ella, who was now standing behind me.

'What do you want, Ella?' I asked, feeling very drained from my conversation with Cal and not particularly in the mood for any more confrontation.

'I'm calling you out, Flick Royale,' she said, a thin smile creeping across her lips. The cafeteria immediately descended into a hush, all eyes watching us in anticipation. I glanced over at Olly, who stood up anxiously when he saw what was going on.

'Ella, I don't know what you're talking about,' I muttered softly.

'Don't you? Miss High-and-Mighty Felicity Royale, friend to the celebrities – I know who you really are, and you're a fraud.' She pointed her bony, manicured finger at me accusingly, and the girls who had come to surround her in support gasped for effect.

'What are you talking about?'

'I'm sure the press would LOVE to know the real reason you've been hanging out with Skylar Chase.' She cackled. 'You just wanted to get your loser *boyfriend* Cal an interview. And you couldn't even do that!'

'That's not why I was hanging out with Sky!' I protested. 'I just –'

'You couldn't get an interview with her because she would never grant an interview to someone who *waits* on her in a hotel restaurant. You claim to be best friends, but there weren't even any photos of you with her at the party. And Ethan Duke hasn't mentioned you ONCE in his vlogs. The truth is, you act as though you're the most important person on the planet, when in fact you have *no friends.*'

. She finished her speech with a smug smile as the cafeteria erupted into whispers. I'd never cried at school before – I'd never had reason to – but with everyone staring at me, my eyes began to grow hot with tears. Ella was right. She had dropped me, Cal despised me and Sky was in a different country – I didn't have any friends. Well, I had Grace but for how long? She'd probably get tired of me too like everyone else. I clutched my fists, desperate not to let myself crumple and cry in front of the whole school. I saw Olly open his mouth to speak and I began to panic – Ella would have a bigger vendetta than ever at me if her ex-boyfriend took my side.

But I needn't have worried.

Because the voice that next rang clearly through the cafeteria didn't belong to Olly. It belonged to his sister.

'Back off, Ella.' Grace was suddenly at my side, her cheeks flushed red. The whole room inhaled at the same time, stunned by this turn of events. It was like a live soap opera.

Ella recoiled at first, but on realising who had dared speak to her like that, she relaxed into her natural sneer. 'Sit down, Grace, this has nothing to do with you.'

'Yes it does. Flick is my friend.'

Putting her hands on her hips, Ella looked bemused and glanced over her shoulder at her group of girls, to share this entertaining moment. But they didn't look as comfortable about the situation as their leader.

'I mean it,' Grace squeaked.

'Grace,' Ella hissed, becoming irritated, 'what are you doing?'

'I'm telling you to leave her alone,' Grace said firmly and loudly enough for the captivated audience to hear. 'She's my friend. So, like I said, back off.'

'Grace, this isn't about you,' Ella said, rolling her eyes, 'this is about Flick and how she –'

'You know what, Ella?' Grace interrupted, holding up her hand. 'No one cares what you have to say.'

More gasps. My jaw dropped open as I stared at her

determined expression. Who was this person and what had happened to meek Grace? Ella was clearly thinking the same thing.

'How dare you!' she snarled.

'Grace,' I whispered out the side of my mouth, as Ella's face grew redder and redder, 'you don't have to do this. I can handle –'

'I know. But I want to.' She turned back to Ella. 'I think it's cool that Flick helps out at the hotel rather than just acting as though she owns it – which by the way she does.'

'Well, technically it's my mum who –'

'Not now, Flick. Ella, you're clearly just jealous of Flick for many reasons,' she said, shooting her a knowing look as Ella's eyes flashed with anger. Or was it fear?

'I am NOT jealous of *her*,' Ella spat.

Grace ignored her. 'Now, if you have nothing nice to say, I reckon this is your cue to leave.'

Ella snorted and Grace stuck her chin out defiantly.

'That is,' Grace continued in a quieter voice, 'unless you want me to carry on. Because I have some very interesting stories from when you were dating my brother . . .'

It was as though someone had slapped Ella round the face. Flustered, she looked behind her, her eyes searching frantically for support, but her cronies refused to make eye contact. They knew a losing side when they saw one. Ella let out a small sob, and pushed past us to run out of the cafeteria and into the toilets. No one followed her. The cafeteria burst into raucous applause as Grace breathed a sigh of relief.

'That felt good.' She smiled, linking her arm through mine. 'Want to sit with me for lunch?'

'You know what?' I nodded slowly. 'I really do.'

So, I hear you're to blame

Oh no, what now?

For my sister's little outburst today. She said it's all down to you?

I wish I could take credit Olly, but I don't think I can. She was amazing. I owe her big time

Well, I wanted to thank you

For what?

For giving her more confidence.
Whatever you said to her at
the weekend, it worked.
My parents and I have been
trying for years to get her to
have a little more faith in herself.
I hated her hanging out with
Ella once I realised what she
was really like

I can imagine. I meant to
thank you by the way. For
your message the other night
before Sky's party

You're welcome. So . . . see
you at lunch tomorrow?

You bet. It's nice having
people to sit with again. I was
getting bored of all those books

Pleased to hear it.

Oh, and Flick?

Yeeeeees?

Try not to start any more rebellions, OK? As much fun as they are, it is only Monday x

I can't make any promises x

TWENTY-TWO

There was a knock on my bedroom door.

'Come in.'

I looked up from my homework to see Mum leaning on the doorway.

'Working again?' She nodded towards the books piled up on my desk.

She had every right to be surprised – it was a Saturday and exactly two days before the end of term, and a week before the Christmas Ball. We had hardly any homework to do and school lessons mostly involved watching Christmas films or working in groups on pointless projects. Considering I had never cared about homework before, I guess it seemed odd to Mum that I would care about it now, when I had a real excuse not to do any. And the lead-up to the Christmas Ball was always my favourite time of year – usually I'd make Ella or anyone who was available come to a hundred different shops with me, and I'd spend all day enjoying their envious looks as I twirled around in various gowns, musing on which shoes would go with each one.

Not this year, though. Ella was still not talking to me. But now, I actually didn't care, because no one was really talking to her either. Things had been way more relaxing without her insisting on being the centre of attention all the time. She still had a few minions worshipping her every move, but since her public telling-off, Ella had been much more low-key, avoiding us like the plague. And, as Olly hilariously pointed out when I was over at his and Grace's house for a movie night, she seemed to strut less when parading down the hallway.

'So do you, though,' he added, when I giggled at his observation.

'Huh?'

'You strut less than you used to.'

'I never strutted!'

'You did.' He laughed. 'You properly strutted.'

'I did not!'

'I'm with Olly on this one, you had a strut going on,' Liam added, throwing up a kernel of popcorn and catching it in his mouth.

'Grace, back me up!'

Grace hesitated. 'I guess there was a teeny tiny strut . . .'

I gasped. 'Et loo, Caesar?'

They all exploded with laughter and Liam began choking on the popcorn.

'What's so funny?'

'You got that so wrong,' Olly said, knocking Liam on the back. 'It's "Et tu, Brute?"'

I snatched the bowl of popcorn from Liam. 'I did *not* strut.'

'Whatever you say, Shakespeare.' Olly grinned, reaching for a handful of popcorn and pressing play on the controller.

I didn't miss Ella but I sort of missed the other person who was still not talking to me. As Cal was older, he wasn't in any of my classes and he mostly kept himself to himself during break times. One afternoon after school, I had been on an errand for Mum, taking some files to Audrey's office and Cal was leaning on the reception desk reading, I assumed waiting for his dad. I took a deep breath and went over to him.

'Hey.'

'Hey.' He looked back down at his book.

Uh-oh. I hadn't thought about what I was going to say after 'hey'. I had no idea where to go from there. Why hadn't I thought this through?

'Did you know butterflies taste things through their feet?'

OK, not the most winning line but I decided to go with it.

'Yeah, I did.'

'Oh. Good. Interesting, right? I was watching *Planet Earth* repeats the other day.'

He didn't reply so I decided I should probably call it a day. Butterfly facts? Really? That's the best I could do? I turned away, disgusted with myself, when he spoke.

'I heard about Grace. Telling Ella off in front of everyone.'

'It was pretty cool.'

'And hotheaded. You must be rubbing off on her.'

'I'll take that as a compliment.'

'Whatever you want.'

I paused, watching him turn the page of his book. 'You know, Cal, I really am sorry. About what I said at the party.'

'It's cool,' he replied, not looking up. 'I get it.'

'Get what?'

'That you were trying to impress whatever his name is. The vlogger.'

'I wasn't trying to impress him. I just –'

'I don't know why you worship that guy anyway,' Cal snorted, turning another page.

OK, no one reads that fast, not even nerds like Cal. He

was totally doing the page-flicking thing to make me think he didn't care and to rile me up. And it was not working. Not one little bit.

'Would you STOP turning the pages like that. It's so annoying.'

(Fine, it was sort of working.)

'My page-turning is annoying you?' Cal finally looked up with this stupid bemused look on his face. URGH he was the worst!

'Look, I do not *worship* Ethan Duke. I like him. He's very nice and hard-working. You have no idea what he's like.'

'I know he cares more about his appearance than anything else.'

'That is not true! If you talked to him –'

'I don't have to talk to him, I can tell from his vlogs.'

'*You* have watched Ethan Duke's vlogs?' I had to admit I was kind of taken aback by this information. Cal was not really a vlog-watching kind of person.

'Just a couple of them recently,' he said defensively, shifting his feet. 'Did he even talk to you properly at the party?'

'Yes!' I lied. 'We had loads of deep and meaningful conversations! About . . . lots of stuff.'

'Sure.' Cal shut his book. 'If you see my dad around, tell him I'm waiting for him outside.'

After that, I wondered why I missed him at all. He was so pompous and self-important. ARGH. He made me so angry, up there on his high horse as though he was some kind of wise old man in a lame fairy tale, lurking at every corner ready to tell you what to do and make you feel guilty about everything.

I decided to try to avoid him around the hotel, so I spent most of the time in the flat with Fritz, attempting to keep myself busy. Which is how Mum found me doing homework on a Saturday morning. 'You know,' I said, holding up *Lord of the Flies* as she leaned on the door frame, 'this book is actually quite good.'

'I'm sure William Golding would value your opinion.'

'I mean it. I'm redoing my essay on it.'

Mum gave me a strange look. 'Voluntarily?'

'Sort of. I got an E on the last one but I hadn't actually read the book then, so Miss Weatherton said if I wanted to have another shot, she'd mark it. I have to get it in before the end of term though.'

'What's with the sudden work ethic?' Mum went to sit down on my bed and I swivelled to face her.

'Nothing.' I shrugged. 'Olly was just talking about *Lord of the Flies* the other day and he said that there –'

'Olly?' she interrupted.

'Grace's brother.'

'I see.'

'He said he thought I should try reading it. Him and Grace are really into books and music and stuff. They're both super-intelligent. I don't really understand what they're talking about most of the time, so it would be nice to join in at least one conversation.'

She nodded. 'Well, tell him thanks from me. So, do you think you might give yourself a break for a few hours?'

'How come?'

'I need your help with something.' She looked at her watch. 'I need you ready to go in five minutes. I'll tell Jamie to look after Fritz today. We have an errand to run.'

A while later we were walking down Bond Street and Mum was telling me about the time she'd had to solve the dilemma of two high-profile guests each demanding the same room.

'The key is to make every guest feel special. Their stay at Hotel Royale is a personal experience. Just like you did with Skylar Chase. You made her feel like she was the most important guest at the hotel.'

'She *was* the most important guest at the hotel.'

'No. *Every* guest is the most important guest at the hotel. Does that make sense?'

'I guess.'

She stopped in the middle of the pavement and looked

down at me with a serious expression on her face.

'Flick, do you know why the Christmas Ball is so important to me?'

'Yeah! Because it's the biggest and most famous social event of the year,' I replied confidently.

'Well, that's certainly true, but it's not the reason why it's so important to me personally.'

'Is it because you love Chef's Christmas chocolate mousse?'

'Another excellent point, but not quite right.' She smiled. 'It's because it's important to you.'

I looked at her blankly.

'When your father and I split up all those years ago around this time, I was terrified that you would start hating Christmas. Did it ever occur to you that the first ever Royale Christmas Ball was that same year?'

I shook my head.

'Matthew and I had the idea to put on the most magical Christmas event we could think of, so you would have a wonderful night. And you did. It's your favourite event of the year, right? Because the Hotel Royale Christmas Ball is all for you. It always has been, right from the start.'

I couldn't believe what she was saying. That her and Matthew had been in it together from the very start just to make *me* happy seemed completely baffling. It was *the nicest thing ever.* I felt so overwhelmed that my eyes began to fill with tears at the thought of it all.

Which is lame but we were totally having a moment so whatever.

'Mum,' I whispered, 'I never had any idea.'

She smiled down at me.

'Well, as you've been so brilliant recently, and as it is, after all, *your* party . . .' She turned round and pointed up at the shop name under which we were standing: Lewis Blume. 'I think we had better go and pick up your dress.'

Good seeing you at Sky's party. Where shall I meet you for the ball?

Hey Ethan! Good seeing you too. Matthew will show you where to go, don't worry. Are you excited?

Yeah, it's going to be fun

He didn't ask me a question

Who didn't?

Ethan. He texted me and then
I replied with a question and
then he answered it

Isn't that a good thing?

No. He's meant to ask me a
question too, so I can reply.
Now I can't reply

Why don't you just ask him
another question?

Grace, I can't do that!

This is all very confusing.
You want me to ask Olly?

NO OH MY GOD

DO NOT ASK YOUR BROTHER, STOP ASKING HIM THINGS

Whoa, OK, I won't ask him! I can't believe Ethan Duke is taking you to the Christmas Ball. You are living the dream

Speaking of the ball, I have something to ask you . . .

Want me to look after Fritz?

No, I wanted to ask if you can come to the ball? You're invited

Hello? Grace? Are you there?

Sorry. I'm in shock. Did you just ask if I want to come to the Hotel Royale Christmas Ball?

Yes, I did. You want to come?

OMG OMG OMG OMG OMG
YES YES YES YES YES YES YES

Haha! Good! And you get a plus one
if there's anyone you want to bring

THIS IS SO AMAZING

I'll call you tomorrow

THIS IS THE BEST EVER. I CAN'T COPE

Night, Grace xxx

I'M LYING ON THE GROUND AGAIN

TWENTY-THREE

The day before the ball, I was sliding down the bannister of the main staircase, minding my own business, when I flew off the end, straight into Cal Weston. We tumbled to the floor, landing at the feet of the London mayor, who very kindly helped me up.

'Nice to see you too,' Cal grumbled, scrambling to his feet, as Audrey escorted the mayor through to the restaurant with a pointed glare at me over her shoulder.

'You shouldn't come round corners so fast.'

'You shouldn't be sliding down the bannister.'

I awkwardly picked carpet fluff off my jumper as he bent down to pick up a folder he'd been carrying. I hadn't spoken to him since the page-turning conversation. He definitely hadn't been getting in anyone's way at the hotel lately – in fact I'd barely seen him in the midst of the Christmas Ball lead-up chaos.

The hotel was now officially a Christmas wonderland, with the big tree up and decorations everywhere you looked. Mum had even put aside an evening to decorate the flat with me, which hadn't happened in years. Sure, our decorations were not quite as elegant as the hotel's, but, in my personal opinion, you can never have too many fairy lights. I'm not sure Fritz agrees. When I turned them on, he got such a fright that he barked madly at them, and now he just sits underneath the mantelpiece for hours, staring at the wires across it suspiciously until I switch them on and the barking begins again. For his (and Mum's) sanity, I've been keeping him out of the flat and he's been chilling in reception with Matthew, greeting guests dressed in his Santa's Little Helper suit. It goes down a treat. A picture on Fritz's Instagram of him in his outfit posing with Prince Harry got 47,000 likes.

Since that response, Fritz had become quite the diva. He turned up his nose at a crisp I offered him and then later on that day I found him downstairs munching on a plate of salmon that Sasha had prepared especially for him.

'I was actually looking for you,' Cal admitted, when I'd finished brushing myself down. 'I didn't quite expect you to launch yourself at me but –'

I rolled my eyes. 'I didn't launch myself at you, you got in my way.'

'I wanted to tell you that I came second. In the journalism competition. Runner-up.'

'That's . . . amazing!'

'I was pretty shocked. I wasn't expecting to get anywhere with it.'

'Cal, that is so great! I can't believe Matthew didn't tell me!'

He looked down at his feet. 'I told him not to.'

'Oh.' I nodded, looking down at mine. 'Sure.'

'The ceremony is tomorrow night. I have to go and collect my award from Nicholas Huntley.'

'Wow, you are going to be so star-struck.'

'Yeah.' He smiled. 'Although, I'm sad to be missing the ball.'

'The ball! Right! That's tomorrow.'

'I'll try to make it for the fireworks. They're always the best bit.'

'They are.'

'Remember how we always used to go sit up on the –'

'Yeah, that was the best.'

He held the thin plastic folder out to me.

'What is this?' I asked, taking it.

'It's my feature. The one I entered into the competition. I wanted you to read it.'

'Really? What is it about?'

'Read it and see. I think you'll like it.'

'Thank you.'

'No worries.' He shoved his hands in his pockets.

'Cal.' I waited for his eyes to come up and meet mine. 'Uh . . . I'm not just sorry about what I said at the party to Ethan Duke. I'm sorry for getting all wrapped up in going to the Christmas Ball and forgetting about . . . well, this. The article. Although, looks like you didn't need me in the end anyway, so that's . . . good.'

'Thanks.' He nodded and then gestured at the door. 'I'd better get going. Enjoy the ball.'

I watched him leave and then pulled the article out of its folder.

Welcome to the Hotel Royale

Behind the Scenes of London's Most Famous Hotel

by Cal Weston

The following evening, Sky met me on the first floor at the top of the staircase. I actually gasped when I saw her, that's how beautiful she looked. She was wearing a strapless, slinky, figure-hugging gold gown with long diamond earrings and a diamond-studded clutch. Her dark wavy hair had been swept to one side, and pinned so that it tumbled over her left shoulder, and she'd really gone all out on the smoky-eye look, with thick black eyeliner and long full eyelashes.

'You look incredible,' she declared, as she held out my hands and looked me up and down. 'Lewis has done it yet again.'

I had to agree that Lewis Blume had not done a bad job. All that measuring and poking me with pins on my shopping trip with Mum had totally been worth it. My dress was emerald green with a high neckline and a full skirt, so that when I twirled, it swished about very satisfactorily. It was the most beautiful dress I'd ever worn and when I had put it on, Mum's eyes welled up – which NEVER happens – and she made an excuse about finding Fritz's Santa hat so she could leave the room. My hair had been curled and pinned up, with some loose tendrils tumbling down around my face, sprayed perfectly into place. I looked a lot more grown up than I felt. The idea of having a date at the Christmas Ball this year, especially such a handsome one, was making my hands very clammy.

I really needed to buy that portable fan.

'By the way,' Sky said, as one of her assistants fiddled with the bottom of the dress, 'I read the article. It's amazing.'

I had left Cal's feature on Sky's bed for when she flew in late the night before, as I knew I'd be so busy helping Mum with last-minute preparations that I might not be able to talk to her about it.

'He really captures the hotel, and all the history of it and the interviews with the staff were so interesting,' she enthused. 'And you get a very special mention right at the end.'

I blushed as I remembered the sentence she was referring to. I'd read it so many times, I'd memorised it.

The hard-working staff are full of passion and pride. The owner, Christine Royale, is the brains of the operation. And at the heart of it all is her daughter Flick – a sprinkle of fun who reminds us what Hotel Royale really is: a home. And, in the words of Dorothy, there's no place like it.

'Right, you're ready to go,' Sky's assistant announced, straightening up.

'One quick thing,' Sky said to me, squeezing my hand. 'I thought you said that the deal had been for him to write the article about me after he'd helped you out at the hotel.'

'That's right.'

'Don't you think it's strange that he'd make that deal?'

'What do you mean? It was an excellent deal.'

'But when I saw Audrey this morning and mentioned the article, she said that the whole reason she'd suggested

Cal teach you about the hotel was because she knew he had interviewed everyone here for the feature he was writing. That's how he knew more than anyone else.'

'So?'

'Why would he then make a deal for an interview with me? He didn't need it. He already had his entry for the competition. So why spend all that time helping you, for something he didn't need in return?'

Her assistant coughed. 'Sorry, Sky, Prince Gustav Xavier III is waiting.'

'WAIT. WHAT?' I blinked at Sky. 'PRINCE GUSTAV IS YOUR DATE?'

'He is so dreamy,' she said, as her assistant checked her dress again.

'But . . . isn't he a bit . . . I don't know . . . ' I searched for the word and failed. 'I mean, he didn't even have an Instagram page until a couple of months ago. And . . . he didn't know how to take a selfie! Who doesn't know how to take a selfie?'

'It's so nice, isn't it?' She sighed. 'He's not into that kind of thing at all. It's such a breath of fresh air. My last boyfriend wouldn't stop taking photos of everything we did. Prince Gustav actually listens when you talk because he's not busy picking a filter.'

'Isn't there a word for that? Old?'

'He's in his twenties, Flick!' She giggled. 'He's just never really got into the whole social media thing. His Instagram page is really coming along, though.'

'Oh. Well, OK then.'

Sky let go of my hand and winked at me. 'Eek! I'll see you down there.'

She elegantly swept down the stairs and I peeked over the bannister to see Prince Gustav wearing a blue sash at the bottom of the stairs looking up at her as though he'd just won the lottery. He spotted me and gave me a salute. I waved and then leaned back, shaking my head.

I did NOT see that one coming.

I waited at the top of the stairs, listening to the music of the band floating out from the ballroom and thinking over what Sky had said about Cal. I guess it was kind of weird for Cal to have made that deal when he'd already decided to do the hotel piece. But maybe he thought the interview with Sky would be better. Or maybe he was just being nice. Or maybe he had jumped at the opportunity to boss me around?

I was so deep in thought about it, I didn't notice Audrey come sidling over from the lift and lean on the bannister next to me.

'Your date is here. Though I can't say much for his timing. He's ten minutes late.'

I jumped to attention, and immediately began straightening my dress.

'Stop fidgeting, you look lovely,' she said sternly.

I took a deep breath, put one hand on the bannister and lifted the hem of my dress with the other so I wouldn't trip, and then made my way downstairs to where Ethan Duke was waiting, looking so handsome, I couldn't believe he was there for me.

'Nice dress,' he commented, holding out his arm.

'Thanks.' I smiled, taking it.

All eyes were on us as we came through the archway into the ballroom, taking a lot of the attention away from Fritz, who, as usual, was the main star of the show, perched on a velvet armchair by the door wearing his Santa suit.

The ballroom had been transformed into a winter wonderland. Every year, the decorations for the ball blow me away but this year it seemed even more amazing because I actually knew the work that had gone into it. Every tiny detail had been planned, each bauble and sprig of holly perfectly placed, and I even made Ethan stop to properly admire the crystal chandeliers – which I'd never taken the time to do before – as I knew that someone had been up a very tall ladder the night before, delicately attaching dozens of red and gold bows to the frames.

Timothy gave us some drinks and we made small talk for a bit, but Ethan seemed restless, as though he'd rather be somewhere else.

'Is everything OK?' I asked finally, giving up on trying to ignore his frantic glances around the room. 'You seem distracted.'

'Yes, sorry.' He sighed. 'I guess I'm feeling guilty about inviting you to be my date tonight.'

'Oh.'

'It's just. I don't –'

'It's OK, you don't have to explain.' I blushed.

'No,' he protested, putting his drink down on one of the tables. 'I do. Everyone I knew was going with a date, and I had no idea who to take, so I just asked you because you'd been so nice.'

'I'm not sure this is making me feel better.'

'I'm explaining this badly.' He sighed, pushing a hand through his hair. 'I guess, I felt you actually listened when I talked to you.'

'Well –' I shrugged – 'you're Ethan Duke.'

'You'd be surprised how few people in this industry really hear what you're trying to say.'

He abruptly straightened up as he saw someone come into the room, not even noticing that in doing so, he'd knocked over his drink onto the table, narrowly missing splashing the Queen of Spain's gown. I followed his eyeline and then everything made sense. His uninterested texts, his 'playing-it-cool' attitude, even that night at the fashion show and the car ride home.

'Does he know?' I asked, placing a hand on Ethan's arm.

'What?' he asked, flustered.

'Jacob. Does he know you like him?'

Ethan sighed and shook his head. 'No. I've never told him.'

We both looked over at Jacob who'd sauntered into the room with a familiar-looking model on his arm. I remembered he had been standing next to Jacob when we'd gone backstage afterwards.

'That guy was on Lewis Blume's catwalk too,' Ethan explained. 'When we went backstage, Jacob told me he was going to ask him to be his date for the Christmas Ball and I had to get out of there right away – by a stroke of luck, so did you. I felt like such an idiot. But you were so nice in the car . . . and I thought it might be fun to come here with a friend, rather than as a third wheel with Jacob and his date.' He looked over at the two of them chatting to Lewis Blume. 'Have you seen that guy? How can I compete?'

'Have you seen *you*?' I retorted. 'You were sculpted by the gods.'

He smiled weakly.

'You should tell him,' I insisted. 'Maybe not tonight, but some time. How do you know that he doesn't feel the same way about you?'

'He would have said before now.'

'He might be thinking the same about you!' I pointed out.

Jacob saw us and waved across the crowd.

'Go say hey.' I nudged him.

'Yeah, I will.' He smiled at me. 'I'm really glad you agreed to be my date.'

'Me too. We'll talk about the vlog later. I'm thinking I could talk about Colin Whittle.'

'Who's Colin Whittle?'

'Oh, he's a *very* important figure in the hotel's history. You wanted to know about that sort of thing, right? There was this ghost and stuff . . . Trust me, it will blow your viewers' minds.'

He leaned over, gave me a kiss on the cheek and made his way through the crowd. As I watched him leave, I was surprised at how . . . OK I felt. I should have been angry, or upset, or disappointed or something. But I felt fine. I think I had secretly known that Ethan wasn't interested all along and at some point I suppose I lost interest too. I did feel a tiny bit mournful about that chiselled jaw, though.

I felt a hand on my elbow and found Grace beaming at me.

'You're here!' I squealed, giving her a hug and then stepping back to admire her pretty pink dress and the delicate rose clips carefully pinned over her hair.

'Is it lame to have brought my brother as my plus one?' she asked, stepping aside to point at Olly coming towards us holding three drinks.

'Hey,' he said, passing one to each of us. 'Wow, Flick, you look beautiful.'

I was so stunned by (a) seeing him there (b) the fact that he'd just called me beautiful and (c) how good he looked in a tuxedo, that I genuinely couldn't scramble my brain together quick enough to reply.

'You . . . uh . . .' I spluttered.

Grace must have noticed I was just staring at her brother, opening and closing my mouth like a fish, as she interjected, 'Mum said he looked like a young James Bond. I think he looks like one of those rubbish magicians at a kid's party.'

'Thanks, sis. Always there to bring up my street cred.' He rolled his eyes. 'Where did your date get to, Flick?'

'Oh,' I began, finding my ability to speak, 'he's gone to say hey to someone. We're just friends anyway. Are you both having fun?'

'It's great.' Olly smiled.

'This is the most amazing party in the world,' Grace enthused. 'Apparently the fireworks start soon?'

I looked over at Fritz, who was being shifted from his chair on to a velvet cushion before being rushed out of the room by Jamie.

'Yes,' I replied knowingly. 'That's the signal. Fritz hates fireworks. Jamie takes him for a snack in the kitchens when they're getting ready to start. The fireworks are amazing. The terrace is a good view but the best view is –' I suddenly had an idea. 'Hey, do you guys want to get out of here?'

'Uh, no?' Grace snorted. 'I am not missing a moment of this party. George Clooney is here and I haven't asked him to sign my arm yet.'

'I mean, to get a better view of the fireworks,' I explained. 'Wait for me in the corridor, I'll be with you in a minute. Seriously, go on.'

I ushered the two of them back in the direction of the door and pushed through the crowd to Sky, who was listening to Prince Gustav telling her and a group of friends about the time he accidentally bought a canoe.

'Prince Gustav,' I said, interrupting his flow of conversation, 'would you mind if I borrowed Sky for a moment? I promise I'll bring her back.'

'Where are we going?' Sky whispered as I led her away.

'I'll show you,' I explained as we approached the others in the corridor. Grace's eyes widened to saucers when she saw who I was with. After hurried introductions – during which Grace just stared at Sky, not uttering one word – I led the way down the hall towards the lift. Just as I pressed the button, Ella and her parents came through the revolving doors. She saw me and froze, midway through taking off her coat.

I don't know if a sudden Christmas spirit descended upon me or something, but seeing her alone, staring at us all together, I felt a wave of sympathy for her. I told the others to wait as I went over to where she was standing.

'Oh, Flick, hi!' Her mum smiled, fiddling with her earrings. 'Don't you look wonderful. You've really managed to find a good colour dress for that hair of yours. That must be so difficult. Did you know it's Ella's first year at the ball? We never miss it, of course.' She waved at someone standing in the archway of the ballroom. 'Oh, there's Sally. I'll leave you girls to chat.'

She swanned off, dragging her reluctant husband with her.

'It's good to see you, Ella,' I began apprehensively.

She didn't say anything.

'I'm really sorry we fell out this term,' I continued,

taking her silence as nervousness. 'I hope we'll all be OK back at school. I know the others would like that too. We're about to go and watch the fireworks. You want to join?'

She looked at those waiting for me at the lift. Her eyes lit up when she saw Sky and for a moment I thought everything might be OK, but then her gaze shifted over to Olly and Grace, and she flinched, returning quickly to her unimpressed facial expression.

'Why would I want to hang out with you?'

'Because we're going to get the best view in the place. Trust me, I know.'

Her lip curled mockingly. 'No, thanks. I think I'll skip the staff quarters, and join the real guests. See you at school.'

She threw her coat to the porter and without another word, she swanned down the corridor and towards the ballroom, patting her coiffed hairdo neatly into place. I watched her go and then ushered the others into the lift, pressing the button for the fifteenth floor.

Grace patted my arm comfortingly. 'You tried.'

'You know what?' I sighed, as the doors shut. 'I have a feeling next term is going to be interesting.'

TWENTY-FOUR

After our first ever fight, Cal found me on the roof of the hotel.

We were eight years old and I had accidentally broken this weird robot thing he'd been letting me play with. He wouldn't let me go near it for weeks because he'd saved loads of pocket money to buy it, but I eventually wore him down and he lent it to me the day of that year's Christmas ball. I was so scared when I broke it, that I hid it in my room and went to the ball with my mum, thinking I'd just tell him later. But he must have gone to get it back before coming to the ball, and he was so angry with me when he found it, that he came to find me and he yelled all these mean things at me. I was so upset, I left the ball and ran back up to the flat. But Mum had locked the door and I didn't have keys, so I went out on to the fifteenth floor's fire escape, and climbed up on to the roof.

Cal came to find me a few minutes later and must have seen the fire-escape door wedged open. He climbed

301

up and sat down next to me as I continued snivelling. He didn't say anything, he just put his arm round me and then the fireworks started and we realised we'd happened upon the best view in the city.

'Look at all those lights,' Grace whispered, when we got to the top and the four of us took in London's glittering skyline in the cold night air. I was pleased they were all impressed because, let me tell you, it had not been easy getting three girls in ballgowns and heels up the rungs of a fire escape.

I think Olly was scarred from the experience.

'That's what I call a view!' Sky exclaimed, getting her phone out to take photos. 'And to think the actual royal family have to make do with the first-floor terrace.'

'How did you find this place?' Olly asked.

Before I could answer, another voice came floating up from the fire escape.

'She broke my robot.'

'Cal!' I cried, peering over at him. 'You're here!'

'Yeah, well, the award ceremony finished and I told you I didn't want to miss the fireworks.'

He climbed up from the last rung, looking very smart in his tux. A warm feeling crept into my stomach as he grinned at me.

'How did you know we were up here?' Olly asked,

as Grace and Sky started the tricky process of sitting down elegantly on the roof in their ballgowns.

'When I couldn't see Flick downstairs, I had a hunch.' He held out his coat to me, which had been hanging over his arm. 'I also figured you wouldn't think to bring a jacket, even though it's December.'

'Thanks,' I said, as he helped me to drape it over my shoulders.

'Where have you been?' Grace asked.

'He's been collecting a big journalism award,' I informed them.

'I didn't win,' Cal interjected quickly, his cheeks turning as pink as his nose. 'I came second.'

'Whatever.' I smiled. 'Your article was great.'

'I can't take all the credit. You were the one who gave me the idea.'

'I did?'

'You don't remember? When you pooh-poohed my Prince Gustav interview, you suggested I write a feature about getting in everyone's way at a hotel . . .'

'The whole thing was Flick's idea? That's cool,' Sky declared, before pouting for a selfie with Grace.

'Wait.' I held up my hands. 'Can we all just focus on the fact that Cal just used the phrase "pooh-pooh" like it was an actual thing?'

'It is an actual thing,' Cal argued.

'Yeah,' I snorted. 'Back in the Dark Ages.'

'I think he can pull off "pooh-pooh",' Olly declared, as Cal nodded appreciatively.

'Out of interest, would pooh-pooh be spelled with an "h" or no "h"?' Grace asked thoughtfully.

'Can people please stop saying "pooh-pooh"?' Sky asked, laughing. 'The fireworks are about to start and all this pooh-poohing is kind of ruining the moment.'

Olly held out his hand to help me sit down in my impractical-for-roof-climbing dress, before offering his jacket to Sky and Grace to share.

'I've been thinking,' Cal began as he sat on the other side of me, 'you *should* start vlogging.'

'Veeeeeery funny.'

'I mean it.' He laughed. 'Seriously. People are really interested in what goes on behind the scenes of a hotel like this one. Now that you've swotted up on it a bit, I reckon you'd be the best person to show it off. Not giving away its secrets, obviously,' he added.

'Cal, are you saying that people might actually be interested in my life?'

'Those weren't my exact words.' He grinned. 'I think it would be fun.'

'That's a really cool idea, Flick,' Sky piped up. 'I'd

watch it. Maybe I'd be lucky enough to have a guest spot on it when I'm next in town.'

'It's a great idea,' Olly agreed. 'I think you should go for it.'

'And me!' Grace said. 'We can help you come up with ideas and launch it after Christmas.'

I smiled. 'OK. I'll think about it.'

As we waited for the fireworks to start, I looked down the line of friends sitting with me: at Sky laughing with a star-struck Grace as they attempted to huddle under the one jacket; at Olly, who was rubbing his hands together to keep them warm, his dark eyes twinkling under those boy-band-worthy eyelashes; and then at Cal, who leaned back on his elbows, before reminiscing out loud about the robot I had broken, even though no one was really listening to him. It really was a weird little crew I had assembled up here.

Olly nudged me. 'What is it? You keep staring at everyone with a strange look on your face.'

'Nothing,' I replied quickly. 'It's just . . . I guess a lot of things have changed recently.'

'Change can be good sometimes.' He nodded, looking out at the view. 'Of course, not all the time. For example, I think that I speak for everyone when I say, we really miss that strut of yours. You should bring that back.'

I whacked him on the arm as he grinned mischievously.

Suddenly there was a loud swishing, whistling noise as the fireworks launched through the air, lighting up the night sky.

'Just like I said in my feature, Flick,' Cal said softly, as we all sat in silence, captivated by the spectacle. 'There really is no place like your home.'

'You know what, Cal Weston –' I smiled, as millions of twinkling lights of all different colours exploded above our heads – 'for once, I might just have to agree with you.'

ACKNOWLEDGEMENTS

Huge thanks to my wonderful friend and agent, Lauren Gardner, who is always there, every step of the way. I am so grateful to you and the Bell Lomax Moreton team, who made all this possible in the first place.

I'm very proud to be part of the Egmont publishing team. Special thanks to Lindsey, Rachel, Liz, Ali and Emily; I have been so lucky to have your invaluable guidance. And to Alice, Rhiannon, Emily and Siobhan who make me look a lot better than I am. Seriously, guys, #SquadGoals.

To my family, thank you for all your incredible support and for constantly cheering me on. You are truly the best and I will always look up to you. That obviously includes the Labradors.

To my perfect godson Sam and the beautiful new additions to our family, Luke and Lily – you bring us all so much joy and laughter. I have hundreds of videos of you all so that I can embarrass you with them when you grow up. Mwahaha.

Huge thanks to my genius friends for your continuing inspiration. Strong friendship is a major theme in all my books. Hey, they say you should write what you know. Couldn't do any of this without you losers, you know who you are.

Thanks to the brilliant team at Stir Coffee in Brixton. Your coffee keeps me writing.

The idea for this book was sparked when I stayed at The Ritz, London – I was in awe of the magic of it all. Special thanks to the passionate team there for inspiring this series.

And the biggest thanks of all to my readers. Without you, I couldn't do what I love every day. I owe you one. As always, I hope this book makes you smile.

THE WORLD FAMOUS
HOTEL ROYALE

Watch out for the next
book in the series...

COMING
SOON!

EGMONT

Q & A with *Secrets of a Teenage Heiress* author, Katy Birchall

Which of your heroines do you have more in common with – Anna from *The It Girl: Superstar Geek* or Flick from *Hotel Royale: Secrets of a Teenage Heiress*?

Taking into consideration the number of embarrassing situations she manages to get herself into, I'd be lying if I didn't say Anna!

I have quite a similar thought process to her, and certainly grew up with the same lack of self-esteem, always worrying over the tiniest of things. Anna's friendship with Jess, who is constantly teasing her, is similar to the relationship I have with my best friends – making fun of one another is our way of showing we care, there's none of that soppy malarkey!

Flick is much more confident in herself, which I think is marvellous, and I've absolutely LOVED writing a character who thinks so differently from me. She's so much fun.

Do you know any real dogs as stylish as Fritz?

Unfortunately, I don't know any who have quite so extensive a wardrobe, BUT I do know a lot of pampered pooches. I was dog-sitting a couple of dogs recently who not only sleep in bed with their owner, but they also have the poshest food I've ever seen. One example was chicken pâté with brown rice and garden vegetables. They are so cute, though, they totally deserve it.

My beautiful Labradors don't get such luxury when it comes to bedding and cuisine, but they are the most spoilt dogs in the world when it comes to love (no, seriously, I will not get soppy about my friends, but when it comes to my dogs, my heart is fully and completely on my sleeve).

Have you ever had an embarrassing experience with a selfie stick?

I don't actually own a selfie stick so no, but I'm going to take a guess and say that I'd probably not be a natural with one. They look very tricky to control and, considering recently on a tennis court I hit myself in the face with my racket when I went to pick up a ball, I think I should probably avoid any contraptions that are even more technical.

Where did the inspiration for Hotel Royale come from?

I've always loved and been fascinated by Grand Dame hotels, and Hotel Royale itself is a real mix of research into my favourites, but the first idea came along when *Country Life* magazine asked me to write a feature on The Ritz London hotel. I got to stay the night there, meet the staff and witness how it all works behind the scenes first-hand. It was the most incredible experience – the team works so hard and the skill is that guests never notice. Everything is simply perfect already, without anyone having to ask.

Like a lot of Grand Dame hotels, there is a real maze of corridors underneath the hotel and some of the staff have worked at The Ritz for years, as have their parents and siblings – like Cal, some of them told me they used to help their parents at weekends when they were little. It really is like a wonderful, big family there.

That made me wonder what it would be like to grow up in such a beautiful, magical and entertaining place as one of London's Grand Dame hotels and *Secrets of a Teenage Heiress* was born ...

What's next for Flick?

A lot of fun and many more glamorous, mischief-making adventures at Hotel Royale – you'll have to read book two in the series, *Dramas of a Teenage Heiress*, to find out!